LOVE WORTH HAVING

KAY KNOLLS

D1228026

BK PUBLICATIONS, LLC

Love Worth Having

ISBN: 979-8-9852093-0-3 (E-book)

ISBN: 979-8-9852093-1-0 (Paperback)

Editor: Kristen Womble, Passkey LLC.

Cover Design: Shari Ryan, MadHat Studios.

Find out more about the author and upcoming books online at www. kayknolls.com

❀ Created with Vellum

Dedicated to my wonderful husband.
You are the love of my life.

1
***

Christina

$\mathcal{I}$ waved goodbye to Kayla, who was now seated in the chair I'd just vacated at the front desk, and walked out of Mass Memorial General without a backward glance. I was happy my shift was over. The setting sun cast an orange glow all around, and the last of the sunlight fell across the walkway leading down to the street. A slight breeze lifted my hair off my face and sent a shiver down my spine. I buttoned my four-year-old peacoat and wrapped the straps around my waist. I needed a new coat, but once again another winter season had passed, and I hadn't made it to The Coat Factory to look for a new one.

The weather wasn't too bad for a March Friday evening in Houston. But the nip in the air had me rethinking the black minidress I'd planned to wear tonight. Well, that and the fourteen hours I'd just spent on my feet running from room to room and being yelled at by a doctor or two as well as a few irate, impatient patients who expected me to do more than was humanly possible. I didn't feel like tugging on the hem of a too-tight dress all night.

I reached up and pulled the rubber band out of my hair, freeing it from the high, pineapple ponytail I'd gathered it into earlier in the day. The throbbing in my head died down slightly as the pressure from the hairstyle eased. My tennis shoes hardly made a sound on the concrete pavement as I walked down the street to the bus stop.

Five minutes later, I was paying the fare and finding a seat on the crowded bus for the short ride to the three-bedroom condo I shared with Nadia and Fey a little outside of the medical center.

God, was I glad we'd gone for the slightly fancier condo not more than fifteen minutes from the hospital where I worked. It made getting to and from the hospital for my shifts so much easier. Neither one of us could afford the rent without the other two. Just another way we had each other's backs.

Guilt had me shifting in my seat as if my butt was on fire. Yeah, there was no way I could bail on them tonight. No matter how tired I was. Fey had been looking forward to Club Yes for days now, ever since she'd cared for the owner's dog and he'd told her he'd added her to the approved list. It was the hottest club in town, only opened a few months ago, and Fey had been wanting to check it out even before her serendipitous meeting with the owner. Nadia had come to terms with the idea of clubbing tonight. And I had been looking forward to it—until the day I'd had that is. I was tired. My feet hurt. I would rather soak in my small tub, then maybe crawl into bed with Charlie McKenzie's latest romantic thriller. It was the seventh in the series. I'd pre-ordered it months ago and had felt a silent thrill numerous times today when I'd remembered it was now available. The exciting promise of reading the book had been like a carrot dangled in front of my nose all day to keep me moving through my shift.

I fished my phone out of my pocket and tapped on my reader app. A bubble of excitement in my stomach made me smile as I stared at the cover of the new book in my library. Quickly, I put the phone back in my pocket. Perhaps I could get out of tonight. I looked out the window and saw that my stop was approaching. I gathered my things and went to the back door moments before the bus cruised to a stop.

I pushed on the doors and exited. The high-rise was at the end of the block. I smiled at Phillip, the evening doorman, as I came closer.

"Good evening, Miss Christina. How are you this fine Friday evening?"

"Exhausted!"

He laughed, already in on the joke. "I don't think that will work, Miss Christina. They're already home, and according to Miss Fey, y'all are going to that swanky new Club Yes."

"I guess we are, Phil." Okay, maybe I wasn't getting out of tonight.

I sighed as I walked through the doors and into the industrial-styled lobby. Made of wood and steel, it didn't invite me to linger. I walked past walls with living grass, straight to the bank of elevators at the far end of the lobby and punched in my access code. Moments later, the elevator opened. I rode up to the tenth floor, to the three-bedroom condo I shared with my very best friends who were my only family. How could I disappoint Fey?

"I'm home." I set my keys down on the long, narrow table in the hallway.

I was hanging my coat up in the hallway closet when I

heard heels on the wooden floors. Turning, I walked down
the short hallway to find Nadia waiting for me in the living
room, her hands on her narrow waist.

"Wow, Nadia, you look hot."

She was going to stop traffic tonight in the body-hugging
black dress she was wearing that stopped just above her
knees. Nadia was the tallest of the three of us, and her bare
legs in those five-inch heels looked like they went on
forever. It didn't even matter that she was wearing her coke-
bottle glasses, her hair was still unstyled, and she hadn't
done her makeup. Not when she had a body like that in a
dress like that.

"You don't. Rough day?"

"The worst!"

"Sorry." Nadia walked over to the kitchen and grabbed a
bottle of water from the fridge. She held it out to me. I shook
my head and waved the bottle away. Nadia twisted the cap
off and took a long sip.

"Fey's been locked in her room all evening. I don't think
she wants to hear an excuse, Chris."

"Don't worry. I just need five minutes."

Nadia lifted an eyebrow but kept her comments to
herself. She was the best sister-girlfriend a girl could have.
Nadia was super supportive, she was smart, and she was
funny. A triple threat. I didn't like to think about why my
very wonderful friend was still single.

I walked into my bedroom and straight through to my
bathroom. My bathtub called to me, and I stared at it long-
ingly, but instead turned on the water in the shower to warm
up while I brushed my hair and stripped out of my scrubs.

An hour and half later, I heard two pairs of heels in the
living room and the muted voices of my roommates. I
swiped a final layer of lip gloss across my lips just as my best

friend—the impatient one—rapped her knuckles on my door.

"Chris, come on! We're not leaving you," Fey declared.

"Yeah, yeah," I muttered, before giving myself one last look-over in the mirror.

Brown-like-dark-chocolate eyes stared back at me. I'd lined my eyes with a black kohl pencil, defining the natural almond shape I guess I had inherited from my mother. My lips looked soft and full beneath the shiny gloss. My high cheekbones were sculpted and well-defined beneath the blush. I'd spent some time curling my freshly washed and blow-dried hair. Now it hung in well-styled barrel waves around my bare shoulders. My eyes trailed down the reflection in the mirror to the black, long-sleeved, off-the shoulder blouse tucked into tight, faux-leather leggings. I wore black heels because I didn't think Fey would let me out the door in ballet flats.

"You'll have to do," I whispered to my reflection. "Ready or not, here I come!" I sang as I walked out of my bedroom and into the living room where Nadia and Fey were waiting. "Whoa, you two look to die for. Are y'all sure you want me tagging along?"

"Don't even try it, Chris! And you look hot too, even if you're not wearing a dress." Fey pulled me in for a quick hug before rushing for the door. "Come on, let's go down. Uber arriving in five minutes."

I caught the look of resignation in Nadia's eyes as she walked by me. She'd flat-ironed her long hair and replaced her glasses with contacts. She was bringing her A game. Yep, we were both at the mercy of Hurricane Fey tonight.

I took my dressy black blazer off a hanger from the closet and draped it over my shoulders, not bothering to put my arms through the sleeves. Moments later we were riding the elevator down to the lobby.

"God have mercy on the fellas tonight. You ladies are smoking!" Phil opened the door for us as we approached. The cold draft of air slapped my face. I was glad for the blazer since the temperature had dropped slightly.

"No guys tonight, Phillip. It's girls' night out," Nadia said in her best therapist voice as she walked by him.

Phillip chuckled. "Then you shouldn't have worn that dress, Miss Nadia."

I laughed as I walked out behind Nadia. I tended to agree. Nadia looked like a runway model.

"You look beautiful tonight, Miss Christina."

"Thank you, Phil." It wasn't true, but Phillip was our biggest fan.

"Don't wait up, Phil," Fey sang as she walked by him.

"It's my job to, young lady. And if you girls find yourself in any trouble, call me, okay? I'll send my brother to get you."

Phil's brother owned a limousine service, and Phil was always offering to send us a car. We had yet to meet his brother, but I suspected that Phil had already told him all about us. The forty-something doorman had adopted us like sisters from another mother.

"Thanks, Phil," the three of us said in unison as Phil moved to open the door of the Uber that had just pulled up to the curb. We piled into the SUV and sat back as the car took off for downtown and the restaurant down the block from Club Yes.

The plan was to eat dinner first and then walk over to Club Yes. It didn't take us long to pull up in front of the restaurant. It was a little after eight o'clock and though the restaurant looked full, Nadia was supposed to have made reservations for us.

Moments later we were being escorted to a table for three in a quiet alcove in a private area at the back of the restaurant. I was grateful for the reprieve before we headed off to the noisy club. The area was mostly empty, except for three hot-looking guys seated at a table. I caught the eyes one of the guys, saw him sit back in his chair and stare as we approached our table.

My legs felt unstable in my heels. I slowed my walk lest I tripped and fell in front of the most gorgeous man I'd ever seen. With wavy, dark-brown hair that prompted a desire to touch, chiseled cheekbones, and a goatee above a mouth that was now forming into a smile, this guy could have been a movie star. Gorgeous was too tame a word for him. I sat down, placed my small purse on the table, and then glanced over my shoulder only to find that now all three of the guys were staring.

Ooohkay.

I felt a spark of irritation. Did they have to be so obvious? I looked across our table at Nadia who, because of her position, would be getting the brunt of the men's stares only to find that my dear friend had opened her rather large menu and was holding it up in front of her face. A look at Fey, who sat on my right, found my other sister smiling at the table of guys, completely unperturbed by their attention.

And there you had it. This right there summed us up perfectly. The drop-dead-gorgeous Nadia, who did everything to avoid male attention; the always-ready-for-a-good-time Fey, who partied as hard as she studied and wasn't in the least perturbed by what went on between a man and a woman. And then there was me—somewhere in the middle, I supposed.

I thought of the Charlie McKenzie novel waiting for me and sighed as I wished once again for my queen-size bed and the down comforter I'd splurged on a couple years ago. Fey's gaze swung to meet mine, and a scowl transformed her face from the let's-have-fun girl to someone who looked fierce enough to rip me a new one.

"Uh no! Not tonight, Chris. And you too, Nadia. Put the menu down. For God's sake, stop acting like prunes. I swear, you two are serious cock-blockers, and I'm not having it tonight!"

I put down the water glass I'd been bringing to my lips with a thud as uncontrollable laugher pushed its way past my lips.

Nadia put her menu down with a laugh that ended on a sigh before she spoke. "Sorry, Fey, but baby, you know my rules. I'm not looking to hook up tonight. So please stop sending them come-hither glances. They look mighty interested enough."

I glanced over my shoulder and my eyes connected with the same guy's again, but he looked away. I felt a jolt of electricity followed by a frizzle of disappointment settling in my stomach. The guys had gone back to eating and chatting. I reached for my water glass, wondering what in the world was wrong with me.

It had been fifteen months since I'd sat across the table from a man on a date and basked in his attention. Fifteen months! I wasn't looking for sex, but I missed the making-out part of dating. That moment when my lips first met his, when his tongue traced my lips or toyed with my tongue, and when his hands pulled me against him. The way he felt solid and strong beneath my fingers. Yeah, I missed that.

I took a huge sip of water. Nadia had the right idea. I wasn't looking to hook up with a random guy tonight either. It was getting tougher to stop at heavy petting, and I found myself questioning just what the hell I was waiting for. Tonight, I was extra tired and slightly horny. My resolve was low. It probably was best to avoid male interaction altogether tonight. Then I could be responsible about the choices I made.

"How's the fellowship application coming?"

Nadia's question had the effect of dousing me with a bucket of ice-cold water. My stomach churned uncomfortably. I shook my head. "I'm still working on it."

"And by that she means she hasn't started it yet," Fey muttered as she continued to peruse her menu as if she didn't already know what she was having. Every time we went out, she ordered the same thing: chicken fettucine alfredo. She carbo-loaded for all the dancing and drinking she planned to do.

"Chris, the deadline is in two weeks." Nadia looked at me with a wrinkle on her brow and her mouth slightly agape.

"I'm working on it. I'll get it done."

"That's what you said last year," said Nadia, shaking her head at me before going back to studying her menu.

"God, Nadia, what gives?" Nadia was the most responsible of the three of us, but she wasn't usually this much of a nagger. I felt my breath hitching in my throat. Heat surged up to my face and a dull ache started at the back of my head.

Nadia set her menu aside before she spoke again. "The nurse's fellowship has been a dream of yours since you started working at Mass Memorial. You're one of the best nurses they've got. You deserve the fellowship, and I bet they want to give it to you too. But they can't, not if you don't apply."

"I'm working on it."

Fey put her hand on my clenched fist, drawing my eyes to hers. She smiled, and I felt the swift anger that had been mounting dissipate. "Let us know how we can help."

I nodded. There was nothing they could do to help me. This one was all on me.

The waiter took our orders and disappeared. Behind me, I heard deep, masculine chuckles that developed into full-blown laugher. I liked the sound of it. It sounded like fun, young, carefree. I wanted that.

I lifted my hand, catching the waiter's eyes. He walked over.

"Scotch, make it a double."

"Now that right there is what I'm talking about!" Fey declared. "Make it two." She smiled at the waiter.

Nadia shook her head and said nothing.

Yep. Fun, young, carefree—that was what I was going for tonight. Tomorrow I would think about the fellowship I wanted more than life itself and my inability to complete the application for the second year in a row.

2

Evan

The bass in the music sent vibrations up my legs, through my body, and out to my fingertips, which were holding the glass full of scotch I'd been nursing all night. I was leaning over the railing on the second floor, watching the countless bodies below me jumping to the sound of Chris Brown's "Turn up the Music." Behind me, Nate and Ty were each dancing with girls they'd pulled from the pit down below and brought up to the VIP section.

Tonight was guys' night out. Normally that meant poker at my place, but Ty had wanted us to experience the latest club he'd invested in.

From my current vantage point, I could see the dance floor, the high-top tables spaced around the room, the bar area swarming with people, and the front entrance. Every so often, the doors opened, and more people walked in. Ty's latest venture was a success. Club Yes was pulsing tonight.

As if on cue, the front doors opened again, and three

girls walked in. A tingle of excitement raced up my spine. I straightened to my full six foot four inches and watched as Bryan, Ty's business partner, walked up to the three ladies and hugged one of them before shaking hands with the other two. He spoke to the one he'd hugged before calling Tammy, the hostess for the second floor VIP section, and turning them over to her.

Excitement coursed through my body as I watched Tammy lead the ladies around the perimeter of the first floor and over to the stairs leading up to me. I tensed as a man stepped in front of the one who'd stolen my breath. Even from this distance, I saw the slow smile that spread across her lips before she shook her head and sidestepped the man, catching up to Tammy and her self-assured friend who was dancing her way through the crowd. Relief replaced the tension coiling beneath my skin. I glanced at the tall brunette with legs that went on for days who followed the other two like a lamb to the slaughter before I once again focused on the one who had stolen my breath the minute she'd walked through the restaurant earlier tonight.

Our gazes had connected at that restaurant, and I'd seriously lost my train of thought. Thinking had been overrated as I'd watched her glide across the room toward me. Hell, breathing had been overrated. Only, she hadn't been coming toward me and the boys. Moments after she'd sat down, giving me her back, I'd still been staring at her like a deer caught in headlights.

Kind of like I was now. I twisted my body so that my back was to the railing as Tammy indicated the large sitting area directly across from ours. The one who was obviously leading tonight slid across the padded bench, loudly ordering a scotch as she went. Her request reminded me of the glass I was holding. I lifted it to my lips and took a sip of the smooth liquid while continuing to watch the woman who made everyone else around her pale in comparison. She smiled her thanks to Tammy and was in the process of sitting when she saw me.

I felt the one-two thump in my stomach even as she grabbed onto the table to steady herself. Hm, interesting. Did she also feel the pull of attraction between us? Then her model of a friend slid in next to her.

"Hey, you guys were at the restaurant tonight," Ty, who had been dancing in the space between the two sitting areas, suddenly announced.

Nate looked up from the blonde whose neck he'd been nuzzling as he grinded against her ass. He stopped dancing altogether and, pulling away from the blonde, walked over to the girls' table.

"Hey!" The irritated blonde stood there, her mouth hanging open, her hands on her waist. When she saw that she'd lost Nate's attention, she grabbed her friend's arm and they flounced away.

I felt a rush of irritation at my teammate's crass behavior. Nate was too self-absorbed to realize he'd just lost major points with two out of the three women at the table he'd approached.

"Yeah, so were you," Miss Self-Assured stated. The other two were watching in silence, in a way that indicated that they were just wing-women and this was all her show.

"Wanna dance?" Nate leaned down and held his hand out.

She stared at his outstretched hand for a couple beats before she slipped her smaller one into his. "I could dance."

Nate pulled her up from the bench and wrapped his arm around her waist. They started moving to the beat.

A minute later, Ty leaned down and whispered in the supermodel's ear. She nodded, though not as enthusiastically as her friend had accepted Nate's invitation. She glanced at the showstopper, who made a shooing motion with her hand. Soon she was alone at the table.

I downed the remainder of my drink, needing the liquid courage before moving over to her. She watched me cross to her the way a tourist would watch a panther on a safari—with open interest just so long as the panther stayed on his side of the wilderness.

"Mind if I sit?"

I saw her eyes go wide before she shook her head. I slipped into the booth across from her and leaned against the padded back of the bench. She really was beautiful to look at.

"I'm Evan."

"Christina."

I murmured her name on my lips, liking the sound of it. Her eyes went wide again, and I couldn't help but wonder what they would look like if she were below me and I was making her come.

"You're beautiful," I said.

She winkled her nose as if I'd said something bad. "Thanks." There was no gratitude in the word. Was she playing coy? Or was it that it wasn't very original? Now that I thought about it, it probably hadn't been very original. No doubt every guy she met led with that fact. She was looking at her friends dancing with my friends.

I wasn't a very good dancer. I was better on the field than off. But the music was seriously jumping, and she was worth making a fool of myself for. "Wanna dance?"

"Not right now, but thanks."

"Wow," I muttered. Struck down! I frowned into my

empty glass. I set it down on the table, then I looked up and found her staring at me, her lips curling up. Great, she was finding amusement at my expense. Not very encouraging.

"It's not you," she suddenly said. "I worked a fourteen-hour shift today and my feet are killing me."

Grateful for the bone she'd thrown me, I asked, "What do you do?"

"I'm a nurse at Mass Memorial."

Really? Now it was my eyes that went wide. Mass Memorial was one of the philanthropies my family supported. It was also one of the best teaching hospitals in the Houston area. Brains and a bombshell body. Damn, she was hot.

"What about you? What do you do?"

Was she for real? I crocked my head to the side as confusion warred with suspicion. I watched my friends dancing with the two girls before focusing on the beauty in front of me again. Was I being punked? Was she setting me up?

First, we'd seen them at the restaurant, seated in the private area not far from our table. Now they were at the same club, in the VIP section no less, seated at the table across from us. Were these girls stalking us? She scowled at me suddenly, and I realized it was because I had been frowning at her this whole time.

"Sorry." I shook my head with a laugh.

She laughed too. It was a musical sound that tickled my chest. "That's okay. And don't bother answering. These questions are always loaded anyway. I mean what if you're in between jobs, or what if you just lost your job today? It's horrible having to answer the prerequisite getting-to-know-you questions, isn't it?"

I shrugged, but I took the out she gave me. I still wasn't sure if she honestly didn't know who I was or if she was just playing ignorant to gain points with me. "Can I get you a drink?"

She shook her head. "I'm at my limit." Then she looked over at her friends again.

Nate and Miss Self-Assured were grinding on each other like long-lost lovers. Ty's model kept a decent amount of space between them. She had a face and a body created for a man's fantasy, but there was something about her that reminded me of Char and brought out my protective side. From the way Ty was handling her, I was pretty sure my friend felt it too.

"Excuse me," the showstopper across from me suddenly said, jumping to her feet.

I stood too. "Where are you going?"

She didn't quite meet my eyes as she answered, "Bathroom."

I watched her to-die-for, leather-clad legs carry her away from me. Her model friend smiled apologetically to Ty before excusing herself and following her. She touched Miss Self-Assured as she walked by, and I watched as the other girl grabbed Nate's shirt, pulling him behind her as she followed her friends down the stairs.

Ty met my eyes for a split second before a grin the size of Montana spread across his lips, and he too was dashing off toward the stairs after the others.

"Fuck me," I muttered to myself before I followed. I was so out of my element. It felt like they were calling plays I wasn't familiar with. Meanwhile, in one of the hottest dance clubs in downtown Houston, the only girl I'd wanted to dance with in years had turned me down and walked away. While the rejection was refreshing, I couldn't tell if it was legitimate or all part of her playing hard to get. And now here I was chasing after her.

Well, technically, I was chasing after Ty, who was chasing after the model, who was chasing after my girl. Tomayto, tomahto. Either way you looked at it, I was way out of my element.

I'd agreed to come to the club with Ty and Nate. It hadn't crossed my mind that a girl at the club might hook my attention the way Christina had. Well, technically, she'd hooked my attention as she'd walked through the restaurant. Whatever. She had my attention. What now?

Nate and Miss Self-Assured soon found a spot not too far away from the restrooms and were back to dancing while they waited for Christina. Ty and Nadia stood at a bar close by, ordering drinks.

I leaned against the wall and waited for Christina to come out. Watching Nate and her friend dance made me want to feel Christina's body moving against mine. I hadn't come to the club tonight planning to hook up with anyone, but one look at Christina and desire was coursing through my blood. I was usually the cool one. Not even a wingman really. More like the designated driver. I wasn't one for hooking up with strangers. Hell, I wasn't one for hooking up period. Now, it was like four years of celibacy was driving me hard and one woman had ignited that storm—Christina. I didn't even know her last name.

She came out of the restroom then. Her eyes immediately found mine, and I saw them go wide with surprise. I could tell she hadn't expected me to follow her. Her eyes were so expressive. Almond-shaped and slanted like a cat's, they also broadcasted her emotions. I liked reading them. Her gaze flitted over to Miss Self-Assured, then to the model at the bar with Ty, before finding mine again. She approached me slowly, one heeled foot in front of the other. Her hips swayed with every step she took. She reminded me of a tigress, sleek and sensual. Her eyes held my gaze. There was an intensity in them that hadn't been there before.

She stopped mere inches from me. Her chest brushed against mine. A trail of heat coursed down my chest and straight to my dormant dick. I felt myself stirring and pushed off from the wall, adjusting my hips so that I wasn't touching her. She lifted her eyes to meet mine. Her chin didn't come higher than my collarbone. She was probably about five foot two without the heels.

"I'm ready to dance, if you want to." Her voice was husky.

Did I want to? Oh yeah, I wanted to. I placed my hand on the small of her back, leading her over to the edge of the dance floor. She lifted her hands, placed them on my chest, and started moving to the music. She was a sensual dancer. More hip action than wild, flailing movements. I matched her moves easily, and I didn't feel like I was making a fool of myself. I liked the way she danced.

I caught the scent of vanilla and coconut and realized it was her hair. I lowered my nose to the side of her neck, stepping closer, and inhaled deeply. She smelled hot, like a decadent dessert I wanted to lick. Jesus! Four years of celibacy was about to go down the tubes tonight, and I didn't mind one bit.

Her hands trailed up my chest before looping around my neck. My hands tightened against her back and pulled her tighter against my chest. I didn't want her to feel the bulge in my pants. I didn't want to offend her, but hell, I needed to feel her against me.

The music tempo changed suddenly. An older, slower song came on. I recognized it from that dancing movie my mom watched when we were growing up. I tightened my arms around Christina and felt her sway against me as the male voice sang of the girl being like the wind. Christina was overpowering my senses. Her smell, the feel of her body against mine, her breath on my neck. She encapsulated me. I was lost in the storm that was Christina, and I didn't want to come up for air.

I lifted my head from her hair when I felt her steps falter. I pulled back far enough to look into her eyes. My heart slammed against my chest before settling somewhere in my stomach. I saw my emotions mirrored in her brown depths.

"I'm going to kiss you now," I warned her.

Her eyes flared in surprise. I watched her nibble on her lip before she nodded. Her tongue darted out to touch the full part of her lower lip. With a groan, I lowered my mouth to hers, capturing her lips, pulling her flat against my body. She parted her lips for me and let me play with her tongue. She tasted of scotch and mint. Delicious. She was delicious.

I felt the bass pumping again, but I didn't hurry our kiss. We stood still, locked together right there on the edge of the dance floor, lost in the world we were creating together.

The first kiss ended, and another began, and then another. I heard her moan and the sound shot straight to my groin. Everything faded to a dull roar. I felt light-headed. If she was willing, I was taking her home tonight. Rules be damned.

The flash of light behind my eyes was disorienting. Then it came again against my closed eyelids. This time, I stiffened. Even in my current distracted state, I recognized that flash. I lifted my head and was momentarily blinded by another flash. I angled my body so my back was to the photographer and Christina was hidden. Another flash. Christ! Where was security?

As if I'd conjured them up, I saw two bouncers moving

toward the photographer. The photographer took one more picture and then darted around Christina and me, heading for the back exit. Moments later, the man pushed through the door and was gone.

"Is everything okay? What was that?"

I focused on Christina, realizing that I was still holding her against me. I dropped my arms and took a step back. I had a pretty good idea of the images the photographer had caught. They told a story all on their own. But when combined with the words from some two-bit tabloid press?

How had a simple night out turned so complicated so fast?

3

Christina

Sunlight filtered through my closed eyelids, and I raised my hand to cover my face. I swallowed the groan that threatened to escape my lips as I moved under my down comforter. My feet were sore, and my legs felt like I'd walked a mile. Slowly, cautiously, I opened my eyes.

I was alone in my bedroom. The only sound was the ticking of the clock on my bedside table. I glanced at it. A little after nine thirty. I pushed the covers down and listened for my roommates. Silence. Either Fey and Nadia were still asleep, or they were no longer in the condo.

Memories of last night, starring one very tall, very broad-shouldered, and so very handsome man rushed through my consciousness. I swallowed another groan. Pushing the covers away completely, I swung my legs onto the carpeted floor and sat at the edge of the bed, waiting for the pounding in my head to subside a bit.

Last night at the club had been insane. I'd behaved in a

way that was so unlike me. Usually, girls' night was GIRLS' NIGHT, as in the girls only. While Nadia and Fey might dance with complete strangers, I was usually okay at the table keeping an eye on our drinks and purses. Evan's brown-like-honey eyes filled with promise crept through my consciousness. The feel of his hands on my waist and then on my face, holding me as his lips moved across mine had me slapping a hand over my face. Evan no-last-name. Yeah, he had turned out to be rather unexpected.

Unlike his friends, whose names I couldn't remember, he hadn't been chatty. Though he'd made small talk with me, he'd been more comfortable watching everyone—Nadia especially.

Yeah, who didn't want to watch Nadia? Seriously, she was gorgeous, like runway model gorgeous. Most people couldn't help themselves. After seven years of being her friend, I usually wasn't jealous about the attention she got, but watching Evan watch Nadia last night had left me with a sinking feeling in my stomach and more self-conscious than ever about my curves. I had wanted his eyes on me. Only me.

Escaping to the bathroom had given me a momentary pause to get my head on straight. Only he'd been there when I'd come out, and it was obvious that he had been waiting for me. I'd promised myself fun, young, and carefree. Dancing with him had given me that for a moment. Until he'd kissed me. It had quickly morphed into heat, raging desire. There had been nothing carefree about his kiss. Intense wasn't even a good word for it. I'd wanted to have sex with him. Me, who was seldom attracted to a guy, and who certainly never led with sexual attraction, had found this guy completely attractive. From the magnetic way he moved with power and grace, completely in control of his body, to the smooth, velvety sound of his voice. I didn't realize I had a type, but now I knew Evan was totally it.

"What the hell are you thinking?" I studied myself in my bathroom mirror. My type? What was wrong with me? One kiss from a guy and I was completely thrown for a loop. I knew nothing about him. He could be married for all I knew. And the weird way he'd reacted to the club photographer shooting a couple pictures for their social media page or something pointed squarely to the possibility of him being married, or having a girlfriend, or someone.

He'd bolted right after the incident, with hardly a word. His friends at least had the decency to excuse themselves before walking away behind him. I'd been left standing a fool there, and when Nadia and Fey had asked me what had happened, I'd had no words for them.

We'd spent the rest of the night in the VIP section, but the guys were gone and none of us had gotten contact information.

I snorted in disgust. Contact information? Fey was right. I needed to start dating. I needed to get out there and get some experience, so I didn't want to sleep with the first guy who interested me and who basically left me hanging in the middle of the club.

Waiting to date until I'd gotten my life together had seemed like a solid plan. Only now it was four years later, and I was still trying to get my life together.

Nadia, Fey, and I had come a long way since walking out of Maxine's home. We'd done what we said we would do. Nadia was a counselor and about to graduate with her master's in psychology. Fey was a veterinary assistant while going to vet school part-time. And I was a nurse. I had no bigger plans than that. We'd each accomplished something. Even this condo was another sign of our success. We'd gone from renting a roach-infested, three-bedroom apartment to this luxurious condo minutes from the medical center. It was a far cry from anything the three of us could have imagined when we'd secretly hashed out our plans in the backyard of the group home we'd all found ourselves in.

Destiny. That's what it had been. We'd connected at a time when we were all three of us alone, unsure, about to age out of a system that hadn't done anything for us. We've made a bond and become our own family. We'd decided to have each other's backs and to do it together. We'd done it!

Well, almost. There was still one thing I wanted to do and had yet to make a move on. The nurse's fellowship offered at Mass Memorial would allow me access to training with some of the best doctors on staff, and it paid an additional stipend of fifty thousand dollars. That was money I planned to use toward a down payment on a three-bedroom house. A house that would be ours. Because living in this condo was wonderful but it wasn't ours, and we could get notice at any time that the owners wanted to do something different than rent to us. Buying a home would offer us stability and security.

Nadia and Fey had their school expenses. I didn't want to burden them with coming up with a down payment for a house. Besides, it was only a matter of time before they left me. My stomach somersaulted at the thought and nausea had me grabbing onto the counter and bending over the vanity until the wave of alcohol in my system settled.

Everyone left me. It was nothing new and nothing to get worked up about. Fey was the most well-adjusted of the three of us, and she had no problems meeting a guy. It was stupid to think that one of them wasn't going to sweep her off her feet one day and convince her to marry him. And while Nadia had some shit in her past she needed to work through, she had chosen the right field, indicating her desire to heal. Nadia deserved the love of a good man, and I didn't doubt she would find it one day. And that would leave me, all alone, in this big condo, trying to make rent by myself. Unless I did something about it.

Love wasn't for me. It hadn't been for my mom either. I wasn't about to have history repeat itself by making the same mistakes she'd made. No, my focus had to be the fellowship and filling out that blasted paperwork.

I wiped the sweat off my forehead and met my eyes in the mirror. "Just do it!"

Pulling off my T-shirt, I turned on the water in my shower, waiting for it to warm up before stepping in. I wished to God I had more desire when it came to filling out the application form. I had no idea why I kept putting it off. I'd meant to work on it since the beginning of the year. Now I was pushing up against its deadline.

My stomach was in knots. I wanted the fellowship. I had plans for the award money. But what if I applied and they didn't choose me? What would I do then? I seriously didn't have a clue.

4

Evan

I grunted as I finished my tenth rep of my fourth set of bench presses. I pushed the barbell up and over into its resting place, breathing deeply to catch my breath.

I'd woken up this morning with a sinking feeling in my gut. Those pictures from last night were going to cause me grief. Rather than waiting around for the shoe to drop, I'd grabbed my gym bag and headed to the stadium, planning to get in a light workout and catch up with some of my teammates.

Now, as I lifted the barbell again and went for my fifth set, I thought about how last night had gone from sexy to screwed in sixty seconds flat. Four years of good behavior down the drain and all caught on camera. It wasn't as bad as last time. Hell, nothing could be as bad as last time.

The barbell suddenly felt too heavy. I pushed it up and back. Worse than the pictures was the fact that I'd opened

Pandora's box with that girl and there was no closing it. I was hanging onto four years of celibacy by a thread. The only thing working in Christina's favor was that I didn't know her last name or her telephone number. I didn't think I would find a photo of her on the club's social media pages. Ty knew better than to put us on the club's social media. He still couldn't figure out how the photographer had made it into the club to begin with.

I was no rocket scientist, but I would bet my last dollar a few Benjamins were involved. The club was new, and Ty had left most of the setup to his business partner, Bryan. So Bryan had overseen hiring the security present last night. Obviously, he'd done a half-assed job. I really didn't know Bryan from Adam, and I probably ought to give him the benefit of the doubt, but I wasn't feeling magnanimous this morning. Not when I was waiting for the fallout I was sure was coming. I did know Ty though, and that photographer had surprised him as much as he'd surprised me.

While in the car on the way back to Nate's house, Ty and Nate had tried to convince me that it was no big deal. I knew better. If this had happened at another time? Maybe. If I'd already closed the MacMillan deal, then maybe it wouldn't matter. As it was, I had a serious problem. A less than squeaky clean image would be a sure turnoff for MacMillan Brothers. One kiss caught on camera! That was all it could take to derail four years of careful planning and good behavior.

My watch vibrated, and I looked down. Jake. I didn't take the call, but I left the workout area, heading for the showers. It was a call best returned in private. Fifteen minutes later, my hair still wet from my shower, I placed my gym bag in the trunk of my Tahoe and got in. When my phone had connected to the car system, I dialed Jake back. "How bad is it?"

"Depends on our response. Where are you?"

"Ten minutes from home."

"Okay. I'll meet you there in twenty." Jake disconnected the call. He hadn't been screaming bloody murder. He'd sounded like he already had a plan to control the situation. Then again, Jake was one of the best agents in the business. He was also my publicist, and he'd taken my image in his tight reigns and hadn't let up once.

Christina crossed my mind. I didn't want to think about her. But it was kind of like expecting the sun not to shine. I had no idea what it was about her that had caught my eye so completely. She was beautiful, yes, but I'd seen beautiful women before. Case in point, her friend was gorgeous, but she hadn't done a thing for me. Only Christina had me spellbound. After the kiss we'd shared last night, and the way she'd felt against me, I wasn't surprised I couldn't keep my mind off her.

We hadn't spent a lot of time talking last night, and I'd be lying if I said my attraction to her wasn't mostly physical. Hell, I didn't know much about her except that she was brilliant and hot. For all I knew, she could be working with the photographer. I thought about it for moment before dismissing the thought. She'd been confused and a bit dazed, unsure of what was happening. No one was that good of an actress, right? Hell, if I knew.

The only thing I was certain about was that I had seen the last of her. I wasn't looking for a relationship. I wasn't even looking for a hookup. Last night was a mistake. It never should have happened. No way was I getting hung up on a random woman I'd met at a club. No matter how intriguing

I'd found her. No matter how pleasurable it'd been to hold her, to kiss her. There was no way.

I saw the first pap when I turned onto my street. Then they seemed to come out of the hedges like a swarm of bees. This wasn't good.

I hit redial. Jake answered just before the second ring.

"Shit, Jake. There's photographers up and down my street."

"I'll call Tom. In the meantime, don't engage them. Say nothing!"

I must have muttered my assent because the phone went dead. I drove down the street slowly. Photographers flocked the car, their cameras going wild. I resisted the urge to slink down into my seat.

Jesus Christ! This was worse than any red-carpet premiere I'd attended with Jake. I wanted to yell at them that there was no story here, but I followed Jake's instructions. The security guard in the guard house must have recognized my Tahoe because the gates began to slowly open when I got closer. Three guards came out of the hut to assist with crowd control, making sure no one slipped past the gates as I drove through.

I stepped on the gas the moment I cleared the gates, rushing down the winding road to my home at the end of the street. I was going to have to send a bottle of M Black to Derek McKnight in apology. One of the unspoken rules of his planned community was no public disturbances. I hated being the cause of that debacle out front, and I couldn't stop the wave of embarrassment that my neighbors were having their Saturday morning routines disrupted because of my carelessness last night.

Christina. Was she experiencing the same thing? Had she been going about her normal routine and been ambushed too? I needed to know she was okay. She'd said she was a nurse. There was no way she would be prepared to deal with this.

Providing she didn't do this, right?

Shit! Right. I hadn't a clue if she was in on this or not. I realized suddenly that it didn't matter. I didn't care. The media wasn't a beast you could control, and even if she had planned this, no doubt she was finding out that she was in over her head. She would need help. Resources like Tom and his security company. Maybe she was responsible for this, or maybe she was just a beautiful girl at a club who'd caught my eye and was about to pay the price. Either way, I needed to know she was okay. I needed to protect her. I shut my eyes and shut the rest of that thought off. That was a slippery slope and not worth going down.

By the time Jake rang my doorbell, I'd had some time to calm down and think about the situation logically. I needed to find Christina. I led him into my kitchen and offered him a cup of coffee. He took it black, sipping on the hot liquid as we moved to the living room. A quick glance at my watch told me it was a little after ten in the morning. Jake was dressed in black slacks and a pressed white shirt. The guy was always well put together, no matter what time of the day it was.

"Tom's sending a guy over. He'll stay with you until this dies down."

I nodded, not about to complain about the bodyguard I'd just been assigned.

"Have you seen it?" When I shook my head, Jake continued, "I emailed you a couple of the articles. Mostly online publications. So far, it's all about you and the mystery girl. No mention of four years ago."

I released the breath I hadn't realized I was holding. Jake

had set up media alerts when he'd come on board so he'd get notifications every time my name came up in the press. I usually didn't care to know because it usually wasn't anything serious that I needed to handle. Jake was more than capable of handling my image. He'd proven that. Now, it looked like he was about to earn his rather large paycheck.

"Let's start from the beginning, okay? Who is she?"

I sat down on the couch next to him, resting my arms on my thighs. "Her name is Christina. She's a nurse at Mass Memorial. I didn't get her number."

Jake pulled out his phone and started typing something. Moments later, I heard the swoosh of a message being sent.

"Okay, Tom's tracking her down. So, what's the relationship between you two?"

"There's no relationship. I met her at Ty's new club last night. We danced." I felt the heat rushing into my face. "Things got a little heated. Next thing I know, a photographer's snapping pictures. He was gone before I could react."

"That was probably for the best. You know the rules. Don't engage. That's my job." His smile was all teeth.

I nodded, feeling steady for the first time since I'd woken up this morning. Jake was a shark when it came to his job, and that was what I needed now. I pulled out my phone. A few taps later and I was staring at one of the articles Jake had sent me.

There, plastered on the screen beneath a headline about me and my mystery girlfriend at Club Yes, was a picture of me kissing Christina. Desire hit me in the gut again. She was beautiful. Only the side of her face was visible in this shot, but what you could see was classic beauty. Long, dark-brown hair, high cheekbones. I already knew her lips were soft and full.

"I'd guess from the looks of that picture, and from the look on your face right now, you like this girl?"

"There's something about her."

"The press wants to know who she is to you. They haven't seen much of your personal life lately. In lying low, when it comes to your personal life, we kind of set up a treasure hunt for them. Everyone's looking to be the one who uncovers your love life."

"Except, I don't have a love life."

"That picture tells a different story. Now, the key is to control the depth of that story. Causal hookups aren't your thing, and they aren't good for your image. They certainly wouldn't land you that lucrative endorsement deal you've been working your ass off for. MacMillan Brothers prefers squeaky clean. And Evan, I don't have to remind you it's in your best interest to do squeaky clean."

Yeah, I didn't need his reminder. I'd enjoyed the relative peace and quiet these last years. Except for a random photographer jumping out at me while coming from the gym or leaving a restaurant with Ty and Nate, I'd been largely ignored. Memories of four years ago, when I'd played a starring role in the press, rose to mind. The flashing cameras staked out at my parents' house, following me everywhere I went, shouting questions at me. I didn't look forward to reliving that circus.

I got up and walked to the kitchen, needing to release some of the energy coursing through my body.

Jake followed me. "We're only a couple weeks from signing the contract. We just need to make sure this unwanted media attention doesn't derail us closing the deal."

"So, what's the plan?"

"How about we give the media what they want?"

"I don't follow."

"You like this girl. Would it be so tough to date her?"

"Feed them?"

"Small bits. Give them something to focus on so they don't go rehashing history. You and Christina are trending now. They're calling her 'Evan's mystery girl.' Let's fill in the blanks for them."

"What happened to not engaging them?"

"We've got to get out in front of this. Control the story out there and the press you receive."

"What if she's not interested in playing ball? Or worse, if she goes to the media?"

"Did she seem like the type who would do that?"

Hell, if I knew. Except, even as I thought that, my gut told me that Christina wasn't like that. I remembered how she'd tried to put me at ease last night when she thought I hadn't told her what I did because I was unemployed or something and she didn't want me to feel bad about it. "What exactly are you proposing?"

"Take her out on a couple dates. We'll snap a few pictures of the two of you holding hands. Nothing more serious than that. We'll ride out the relationship for a couple weeks until something else takes precedence."

"Christina's a nurse. She has a life of her own. I'm not sure she'll want to be part of this circus."

"You can make it worth her while."

"Pay her?"

"Reimburse her for the time she spends with you."

"Jake, I don't know about this."

"Trust me. Let me do my job. I promise you, by the time this is all over, you'll have your endorsement deal. And this will be nothing more than old news."

"Any chance this will blow over on its own?"

The look on Jake's face said it all. It might, but until then I would be at the mercy of a media that was looking for more info to feed the public's current fascination with me. Jake wanted to keep them focused on the here and now. If it was a romance they were looking for, then it was a romance they should get.

"Okay." I nodded. "How do you plan for us to do this?"

Jake smiled and indicated the chair behind me. I sat down and listened as Jake outlined a solid game plan that made me think he'd been working on this all morning instead of the half hour he'd been in my house.

5

Christina

$\mathcal{I}$ was running the vacuum in my bedroom when I heard the front door opening. I shut it off and went out to greet Fey and Nadia. One look at Nadia's grim mouth and the two venti-sized coffees she held in her hands and I knew something was up.

Fey set her keys down with a clang and rushed to me, her heels clicking on the wooden floor. "You're going to want to sit down for this."

She caught my hands and pulled me down on the couch next to her. Nadia sat on the coffee table in front of me, handing me one of the lattes.

I physically recoiled from her outstretched hand. Lattes were Nadia's thing. Her comfort food. Some days, I suspected it was her only food. Her giving me one was an act of love, or compassion, or fortitude, or something. "What's going on?"

"Take it. It's hot."

I took the coffee cup and then brought it to my lips. Vanilla latte. Delicious. It was better than the cup of black coffee I'd had this morning to get myself going. "Thank you. It's delicious. Now what gives?"

"Remember that guy you were dancing with last night?" Fey asked without further prompting. Her golden blonde hair was falling out of the messy bun she'd pinned it up into after her shower this morning. Wet strands had dried into soft curls around her face. She looked fresh and gorgeous with just the hint of foundation—despite the fact we'd had a late night last night.

"Evan?"

"Yes! He's Evan Kennedy."

When I shook my head in confusion, Fey continued. "Of the Houston Texans."

"Football?"

"Yes, as in he's a star player. And he's loaded! As in billionaire loaded. His father owns Kennedy Enterprises."

Realization knocked me back against the couch. So that explained the photographer snapping pictures of us last night.

"Is he married?"

"No."

"Does he have a girlfriend?"

"I don't think so. Most everything I read seems to be focused on the fact that he was finally dating someone."

I took another sip of my coffee to avoid feeling like I'd just been run over by a truck. Thank God he wasn't a married man, but he was still in a relationship. Taken. So that further explained his reaction to the photographer snapping pictures of us making out. He'd been caught. Red-handed.

My stomach churned with a combination of expensive coffee and dread.

I met Nadia's eyes and saw the sympathy there. She shook her head even as she spoke. "It's you they think he's in a relationship with."

"Wait a minute. What?"

"You're famous, girl! You're trending all over the internet. You and Evan-billionaire-Kennedy."

Fey was smiling like it was Christmas morning. Nadia was staring at me as if I'd just lost my puppy.

"What the hell?"

Nadia set her coffee cup down and pulled her cell phone out of her pants pocket. She tapped-tapped on the screen a couple times before holding the phone up to my face. I grabbed her cell and zeroed in on the headline on the screen.

Evan Kennedy Steps Out on the Town with Mystery Girlfriend!

Beneath the caption was a picture of Evan and me locked in one of the heated kisses we'd shared last night. I was draped all over him, and he was bending down, his lips on mine, his hands on my back melding me against him. No one looking at that photo would think we were strangers who'd just met that night. But we were. And I hadn't had a clue who he was.

"Mystery girlfriend! That's you, babe!"

"Fey, stop. You're acting like she won the lottery. This is bad."

"How is this bad?"

"It's all over the internet! News like this is only going to cause people to want to find out who she is. And when they find out that Christina isn't his girlfriend, what's that picture going to do for her reputation? For the fellowship selection committee?"

"Shit." The word was a whisper leaving my lips.

Nadia was right. There was an unspoken moral behavior aspect to the fellowship in that all the nurses who'd received it had been of high standing in the community. They were mostly all twice my age, married, or in a committed relationship. Certainly, none of them had been plastered across the internet for making out with a random they'd met just minutes before.

This had far-reaching consequences. The good thing was that he wasn't a married man. Or in a relationship, it appeared. There was no law against kissing a man, even a stranger...a hot stranger...famous football player, billionaire stranger. The operative word was probably player. Only, I didn't think Evan was a player. I remembered how he'd looked surprised when I'd shot down his attempt to make small talk at the table. And how relieved he'd looked when I told him I didn't really need to know what he did for a living. Shit! I'd thought he was unemployed. He didn't strike me as a famous billionaire. He'd seemed like a quiet guy, more content with watching his friends have fun on their night out than trying to score himself.

When he'd asked for permission to kiss me, I'd all but begged him to. Because the butterflies swarming in my stomach all night from the feel of his body against mine had demanded freedom that only came from his lips on mine.

"It's all a moot point." I stood abruptly, sidestepping Nadia and Fey. I walked across the living room to the floor-to-ceiling sliding door. I pushed it open and let the cool breeze blow across my face.

It was sunny outside. I could see the park in the distance, and I could just make out the people running or playing there. Carefree, fun! My stomach rolled over again. It was the stress. I hadn't drunk that much last night. It had to be the anxiety over this entire situation.

"He doesn't know who I am any more than I knew who he was. We didn't exactly exchange contact information last night. This is all a moot point. It's going to blow over."

"This isn't something you just ignore and it goes away. The media's not like that. Not when the story's this hot. Something about you and this guy and that image. It's gone viral, Chris. You're wrong if you think this is going away."

"So, what am I supposed to do?" I turned to face Nadia, a little annoyed with her. She was probably right, but now I understood where the phrase "don't shoot the messenger" came from. I dialed back my annoyance, determined not to take it out on her. Nadia's demeanor made it entirely too easy for her to be the punching bag. None of this was her fault. She wasn't the one who'd made out with a stranger in the middle of a night club. Could I be any more cliche?

I spent the rest of the day hiding in my room. Nadia and Fey went out for a bit and came back with a cobb salad for me. I ate it in my room. Yes, I was avoiding them. But I didn't want to see the worry in Nadia's eyes or the sympathy laced with excitement in Fey's.

Mostly, I just needed the quiet to process the huge mess I'd stepped into. Most women went out for girls' night out and didn't end up with their night's indiscretion plastered all over social media. The only thing I had going for me was that the camera hadn't really caught much of my face. The photographer had only gotten my profile. And Evan's large hands cupping my cheeks had blocked out most of that profile. It was going to be very hard to pin the girl in the picture down as me. I just needed to keep my head down and pray that this would all blow over soon.

The doorbell chimed. I glanced at the clock. Who could be ringing our doorbell at seven o'clock at night? I heard muted voices in the living room. A couple of the voices sounded male. I pushed the covers away and jumped off my bed. I paused at my dresser to run a brush through my hair before opening my bedroom door and peeking out.

Evan Kennedy stood in the middle of my living room. He was dressed in jeans, and a brown leather jacket covered his white T-shirt. He took his black baseball cap off and held it loosely in his hands.

"Hello, Christina. Can we talk?"

I glanced at the tall man standing next to Evan, then at Nadia who was standing with her hands folded across her chest and a pissed-off expression on her face. Fey was seated on the couch, her feet tucked beneath her, and her eyes focused on us, like she was about to watch her favorite movie.

"Privately?" Evan added.

I frowned. I didn't mind speaking with him, but privately might be a bit of a problem given that my friends didn't look inclined to go to their rooms. I looked at the balcony behind me and was about to suggest that we go out there when Nadia spoke. "I don't think that's a good idea, Chris."

"She's right. Anyone with a long-lens camera can get a shot of you two on the balcony," said the man who'd accompanied Evan.

"I was referring to her being alone with him."

"You think the media's after Christina?" Fey asked.

"How did you find me?" I asked the question that was foremost on my mind.

Two red spots bloomed on Evan's cheeks. He shrugged his shoulders and put his cap back on, pulling the brim down. His hands disappeared in his back pockets.

"That was my doing actually." I looked at the other man again. I wanted to ask him just who he was since he seemed to be doing all the talking for Evan, but I bit my tongue and tried to keep a cool head. As if he knew my thoughts, he added. "I'm Jake Bassett. Evan's agent and publicist."

"Christina Hart." I shook the hand he extended.

"Christina, it's a pleasure to meet you, though I wish the circumstances were different."

I glanced at Evan and couldn't look away from his honey-brown eyes. He was still standing there with his hands in his pocket, watching me. He looked taller and bigger this morning than he had last night. Maybe it was because he was dressed so casually, or maybe it was because I now knew he was a football player and I could see how well he fit the stereotype.

After a moment of silence, Evan finally spoke. "Did you know who I was last night?"

"No."

"But you do now," he guessed.

"Yes."

Nadia took a step forward so that she was standing by my side. "Of course, she does now. Her face is plastered all over the internet. The point is, you knew who you were, and you should have warned her that dancing with you was hazardous to her private life."

Evan flinched. I placed my hand on Nadia's arm, hoping she would stop. Jake spoke, drawing all eyes to him. "Last night was an unfortunate event, and not the norm for Evan. It's my job to help you two navigate this with as little fallout as possible."

"Do you have a girlfriend? Is that it?"

Evan took a step toward me. "No. I don't. Can we please talk—alone?"

He looked so uncomfortable I felt sorry for him. This was the second time he'd asked to talk with me. I couldn't turn him down. I nodded and turned to my friends.

Nadia rolled her eyes and walked away, heading for her bedroom. Fey uncurled herself from the couch. "What about him?" She pointed at Jake.

Evan turned to him. The two of them must have had a plan walking in here or they knew each other well enough to communicate silently, because a moment later, Jake was pulling a paper out of the inside of his sports coat and setting it down on the counter before he turned and walked out of the apartment. Satisfied, Fey disappeared to her bedroom.

There was silence all around us. I suspected Fey was standing by the door with her ears pressed up against it. Nadia was probably sitting at her desk with a textbook and a notebook open in front of her, doing her best to lose herself in her assignment. And me? I was busy just trying to hold it together.

My heart raced, causing my breath to come faster and harder. I wasn't sure if my shortness of breath had to do with the situation I'd suddenly found myself in, or the man standing in front of me.

"I'm sorry." Evan broke the silence with his smooth-as-velvet baritone.

Suddenly, I saw what all the media fuss was about. Evan was handsome as hell. He was literally larger than life, with his height and his broad shoulders. But that was just the tip of his attractiveness. It was his dark, wavy hair, his brown-like-honey eyes, and his wide, kissable lips. He was the most handsome man I'd ever seen in my life, and he was the only man I'd ever had such a strong physical attraction to.

"It's not your fault, is it?" I took a step toward him before

I realized what I was doing. I sat on the couch instead and tucked my legs beneath me. A moment later, he sat on the couch next to me. I turned to face him.

"According to your friend, I should have been wearing a hazardous sign."

"Nadia's just being protective. She doesn't mean anything by it."

"Yeah, I get that. Jake's the same way."

I nodded. I had seen that too. Jake might work for Evan, but it was obvious they were friends as well. I'd had people do things for me because it was their job, and then I'd had people do things for me because it was their job *and* they wanted to. It made all the difference.

"I'm not sorry I kissed you though."

I shivered at his words. He saw my reaction and smiled a slow smile that started at one corner of his mouth and made its way to the other. It was cocky and sweet at the same time, and it made me want to kiss his lips again.

I gave in to the desire swirling between us and admitted the truth. "Neither am I."

"I don't want that to change, which is why I came. Look, I know you're not used to the media and how crazy they can get. The attention, the frenzy to get the story, it can all be quite overwhelming. I don't want you to have to go through that alone."

"Why?" He frowned, and I continued. "Why do they care who you're dating? Or what you do? I mean, I thought the media went after celebrities more than they did athletes? No offense."

"None taken. Let's just say that I usually don't find myself in the spotlight. My fans are beside themselves at the possibility that we're dating, and there's a curiosity there to know more about you. It's driving the paparazzi to get that money shot."

"Money shot?"

"Pictures of you and me. Pictures of you and your girls. Or your family and friends. You at work. Just anything that sheds light on who you are and what you're about."

I thought about my life now, my life six years ago, my life thirteen years ago. My skin crawled at the thought of all of that exposed for anyone to read, to see. "How do you live like that?"

I saw some of the tension go out of his shoulders at my question. He shook his head. Didn't quite meet my eyes when he answered, "It comes with the territory I signed up for."

"You didn't sign up for this." I touched his arm. "No one should have to live like that, no matter their job."

He placed his hand over mine. His hand was big and covered mine completely. He was warm. Alive. He felt good. I lifted my gaze and found him staring at me. He swallowed and his Adam's apple bobbed.

"Jake has an idea to control the media and the level of invasiveness in your life."

I pulled away from him and folded my hands in my lap. "I'm listening."

"We can control the narrative by providing the media with what they're looking for, but on our terms. If we were to go out on a couple dates, give them a couple opportunities to shoot us together, to run a couple stories about us, then it's only a matter of time before they lose interest or another story comes along and makes us old news."

"You want us to start dating?"

"It would be a pretend relationship of course. But, yeah, a few dinners, attend a few events I have coming up."

"You want me to pretend to be your girlfriend?"

"I would make it worth your while."

"Oh, I'm sure." I pushed my hair away from my face, tucking it behind my ear. "Evan, any girl would be happy to be your girlfriend. I'm sure there's someone else you can ask to fill my role."

"I can't run the risk of that blowing up in my face. What if they found out she wasn't you? I'd rather not have an angry press on my hands."

"So, the alternative is you and I dating?"

"Three weeks. Fifty thousand dollars. I'll give you twenty-five now and twenty-five at the end."

Was he serious? I stared at him, looking for a hint that he was pranking me but saw none. Fifty thousand dollars? It was the exact amount of the fellowship award. It was a down payment for my house, with extra for my emergency fund. It was a game changer. I didn't know if I should be excited or insulted that he'd just offered me that money. "You're paying me to date you?"

"I'm paying you for your time. I realize you have a life, a job, friends. I'm asking you to turn it all upside down for a couple weeks. And I would want your complete confidentiality, of course. I'm hiring you, and so I'm paying you to compensate you. It's all aboveboard."

"And that kiss we shared? Are you expecting more of that?"

He smiled again. "Not for the fifty thousand."

I felt the warmth flush through my cheeks. What the hell? Who was I kidding? He was right. I would kiss him again for free. We'd barely been in each other's company before we'd locked lips. If we started dating, pretend or otherwise, how soon before the chemistry between us led to another kiss, or even more? But he wasn't expecting me to put out just because he'd be giving me fifty thousand dollars.

"We kissed even before you knew what I did for a living. It's not my money that makes me attractive to you."

Oookay. Handsome and cocky. I took a moment to appreciate the tingles flowing through my body. Yeah, Evan Kennedy did it for me.

He was right. I didn't watch football. I wasn't even sure if I liked the game. I did like him though. He came from a very rich family, but he didn't act like I imagined a billionaire would. He seemed like a nice guy. He was sure about himself. Could I handle this? If I were wanting to date someone, he would probably be a good choice. If I wanted to date, that is.

"I'm sorry." I stood up and walked away from him and the couch. "This is...more than I can process right now. I'm not wanting to date you or anyone right now. I have my hands full with my job and stuff I'm trying to get settled. I don't have the time for this. I don't have the time to participate in this charade. I'm sorry. My answer is no."

"Is it the money? If I offered you more money, would that help to make this worth your while?"

"No, it wouldn't. It's not about the money. It's about my privacy and my life and the plans I have that don't include dating."

"So, you don't date?"

"No. I don't."

"Neither do I. Hence my current situation."

Curiosity got the best of me. "Why don't you date?"

"Why don't you date?"

"Touché." I smiled. Yeah, I really liked this guy. "You're better off finding someone else to be your mystery girl."

"I doubt it."

"Goodbye, Evan." I held my hand out to shake his once more. "It was nice meeting you."

"So, there's nothing I can say to change your mind?" He held onto my hand.

I shook my head. He lifted my hand to his mouth and, at the last moment, he turned my hand so that his soft lips met the inside of my wrist. Heat slammed into the pit of my stomach and pooled between my legs. Good God, that was hot.

I pulled my hand away from him before I combusted right there in the living room.

"Goodbye, Christina."

He turned, picked up the paper Jake had set down on the counter and walked out of the apartment, closing the door softly behind him. I felt as if he'd sucked all the air out of the apartment. I sat on the couch, afraid my legs would give out on me.

"Breathe." I uttered the word in the dead living room.

I took a deep breath, and another, and then another. It did nothing to dissipate the sinking feeling that I'd just lost something.

6

_____

Christina

*T*he press found me five days later. I was standing behind the nurses' desk when I suddenly noticed that most of the people in the waiting room were taking surreptitious sneak peeks at me. Most of them had their phones out and were looking from the screen to me.

Suddenly, a woman who'd brought her son into the ER—for what I was sure would amount to nothing more than strep throat—pointed her phone at me. I frowned, wondering what in the world she was doing. Then it dawned on me that she was taking my picture. As if she'd set off a chain of events, more people lifted their phones and began snapping pictures of me.

"What in the world's going on?" One of the doctors close by muttered as he set his clipboard down on the counter in front of me.

I bolted for the doors leading back to the emergency rooms, sure that the crowd couldn't follow me. I leaned against the wall and took a deep breath. I opened the news app on my phone and only had to scroll down to the second story before I saw it.

"Oh my God!"

Evan's Mystery Woman Revealed!

There was a picture of Evan and me staring straight at the camera. Evan's hands were on my shoulders and, though we were still standing in front of each other, we'd both turned to the photographer. The shock on Evan's face was plain to see. I looked confused and a little dazed. I remembered the moment when we'd both looked at the photographer before Evan had moved, blocking me from the camera. A moment later, the photographer was gone.

They had a photo of me. They'd had it all along. But they'd gone with the mystery woman angle to hype up the public. Now, this story identifying me would mean so much more to the press and would have so much more of an impact.

My hands were shaking as I put my phone back in my pocket. I was working the front desk today, but I didn't dare go back out there. I leaned against the wall. What should I do? The impulse to run and keep running was strong. I took a deep breath. I couldn't leave. It was Thursday midafternoon and, while it hadn't been busy, I still had three hours left on my shift. I'd never left work mid-shift before. I'd never even called in sick. I couldn't be so irresponsible as to leave halfway through my shift, no matter what was going on.

This was my job. My life. How could I submit my application for the fellowship the same week I ran out on my shift? That wasn't excellent job performance. The fellowship was everything I'd been working toward for the past four years. I wasn't going to let the opportunity slip away because of one bad photograph.

I pushed myself off the wall and headed back into the front lobby. It felt like all eyes landed on me the moment I walked through the doors.

"There she is."

"It's her."

"Are you sure?"

"Yes! Look it's her."

I ignored the whispers and walked behind the desk. I smiled at Amanda and grabbed the ringing telephone to avoid her questions. After the call was finished, I reached for a chart and got busy updating the records. I kept my head down and tried to ignore the stares and the whispers.

Not enough time had passed before a woman approached the desk. "Christina?"

I looked up at the sound of my name. A woman I'd never seen before was standing in front of me.

"Is this you?" She jabbed her phone in my face. I saw my image staring back at me.

The room was silent. I looked around. Everyone was watching me, waiting. I felt light-headed. My heart beat violently against my chest.

"Did you need something, ma'am?" Amanda stood up.

The woman went back to her seat. Amanda glared at me. I felt my cheeks burn. Okay really, what was wrong with these people? Even if I was Evan's girlfriend, seriously, what in the world was wrong with them? Was the guy a god? Was he the most eligible bachelor in the country? They were acting like he was a movie star or something.

"Can I get a picture with you?" A girl who couldn't be more than sixteen was standing in front of me. She smiled as if it was quite normal to ask for a picture. I looked behind her and saw a woman who must be her mother sitting in one of the chairs, her phone up. Clearly, she was video-taping the exchange.

"No. I'm sorry, I can't do that."

The girl's smile fell. She looked confused for a moment, as if she hadn't expected me to say no. Then she looked mad. "Whatever," she muttered as she walked back to her mom.

What was wrong with these people?

Amanda and I exchanged another glance. This time, I thought I saw sympathy in her eyes. "I'm calling security." She picked up the phone. "We've got a problem here." I heard her say. "We need extra security in the lobby, stat."

I wanted to crawl under the table in mortification. A few minutes later, two security guards and the chief of nursing walked into the lobby. Chief Nancy stopped near to the doors and signaled for me.

It felt like a walk of shame as I got out from behind the front desk and walked over to her. I followed her through the same doors I'd escaped through earlier. She didn't say a word as we walked to her office. She shut the door behind me and indicated the chair in front of her desk. I sat, folded my hands in my lap, and waited.

"You've caused quite a commotion today. Care to explain?"

"It wasn't on purpose." I felt my embarrassment give way to irritation. Chief Nancy was usually quite understanding. Certainly, she didn't think this was my doing.

"This is a hospital. We do serious work here. This type of distraction can be dangerous. I'm sorry, Christina. I'm going to have to ask you to go home."

"Are you firing me?"

"No, of course not. Just take the rest of today off. Report

to work on Monday. Hopefully, this will have blown over by then. If not, I'm sure we can figure something else out. This attention, however, just won't work."

I wanted to scream and yell and declare that I wasn't going anywhere. But I liked my job, and I enjoyed working under Chief Nancy. I'd always found her to be stern but caring. I hated being on the receiving end of her discipline.

"Go gather your things. I'll have one of the guards escort you out." She held up her hand when I opened my mouth to protest. "Only for your protection, of course."

There was so much that I wanted to say. But I found myself nodding and leaving her office quietly instead. I stuffed my clothes into my tote, not bothering to change. I ripped the photograph of Nadia, Fey, and I off my locker door and put it in my tote as well. Then, I didn't know why I'd just done that. It wasn't like I'd been fired. Except, in that moment, it felt like I had been.

I'd thought I could do my job still and that if I held my ground, I could get through my shift. I hadn't counted on people approaching me while I was at work! I sat on the bench in front of my locker. I didn't know if I could make it home without being harassed. I shuddered at the thought of getting on the bus. I reached for my phone to call an Uber and saw that I had two missed calls and a couple text messages. They were from a number I didn't know. I clicked on the last text message.

Christina. It's me again. You're not answering your phone or texts. I don't know if you've seen the news today. DO NOT GO OUTSIDE! Call me. Please! - Evan.

I pressed his number without a second thought.

One ring later, he answered. "Christina?" My eyes blurred at the sound of his baritone. "Christina?" I heard the concern in his voice. Tears splashed on my cheeks. I tried to stifle the sobs threatening to break through. "Tell me where you are, baby."

"I'm at work. They want me to leave. They said I'm too much of a distraction."

"Don't cry, baby. It's going to be okay. Where are you now?"

"The locker room."

"Stay there, okay? I'm sending someone to pick you up. His name's Nigel. He'll be there in fifteen minutes. He'll pick you up on the third floor of the garage. Stay in the locker room. I'll call you when he's there."

Twenty minutes later, Evan called again. My ride was in the garage. I walked out of the locker room and found a security guard waiting to escort me out of the building. I knew it was for my protection, but I still felt like I was being escorted off the premises. I told the guard where I needed to meet Nigel and then walked quietly with him to the garage.

Moments later, the guard was handing me off to Nigel, who was waiting for me when the elevator doors opened. Nigel was almost as tall as Evan, though much leaner and with dark-brown hair. I climbed into the back of the black Tahoe and closed my eyes. Minutes later, we were pulling out of the garage and away from the hospital. I expected it to be a short drive to my condo, and I sat up suddenly when I realized we were going in the opposite direction.

"Evan asked me to bring you to his house, Miss Christina." Nigel answered my unasked question. "He thought it would be better for you, and safer for your friends, if you didn't go back to your condo just yet."

I met Nigel's eyes briefly in the rearview mirror before he returned his gaze to the road.

If the hospital had been crawling with people trying to

take my picture, I could just imagine what outside the condo looked like. "I have to warn my friends."

"Evan's also sent a car to pick up Miss Nadia and Miss Fey, and their driver will make sure they get home safely."

Relief washed through me, and I felt my body go limp. I sank deeper into the luxury leather. Evan had taken care of everything. It was comforting to not have to deal with it for a while.

We drove for twenty minutes before Nigel turned onto a much quieter street. I sat up straighter, looking out the window for the street signs. I soon recognized the exclusive gated community that existed on fifteen thousand acres. Nigel slowed down at the security gate. A guard came out, and Nigel gave him our names. The guard glanced at me briefly before nodding and wishing us a good day.

We drove through the open gates, and I got my first look at the prestigious McKnight Grove. The streets were wide and lined with tall trees, with hardly any cars parked on the side. Each property had its own driveway that led to a huge mansion or tall iron gates that hid the house from street view. I knew that the homes started in the lower millions. The planned community had been developed by the McKnight family, and the custom-built homes were owned by billionaires. And Evan lived here. To think I'd thought he was jobless.

Nigel drove down the winding street to a huge Mediterranean-styled home behind wrought-iron gates. The property was fenced all around. The front gates swung open, and Nigel drove up the circular driveway and then turned right, driving through a courtyard. He pressed the garage button on his visor and large wooden doors swung upward. He drove the black Tahoe into the large garage that could easily hold four cars. There was another black Tahoe and a white, two-door Maserati sports car parked in the other spots.

Moments later, my door was opened from the outside and I was staring into Evan's handsome face. Heat warmed my stomach and pooled between my thighs. I looked away from him under the guise of collecting my tote bag. He stepped back and helped me out of the car. I followed him through the garage to a side door that led into the house.

We entered just inside his foyer, from where I could see the intricate glass and metal front door. The foyer was beautiful and open with white tiles and high ceilings. Paintings hung on the white walls. There was a dining area with a large table and chairs on one side. On the other side was a room that appeared to be either his office or a den. A wide, curving staircase led to the second floor.

"This way," Evan said, leading the way into the room across from the dining area.

It was a library! The room was designed in wooden oak-colored panels and floors. It was two stories high. Built-in shelves lined the walls, and there was a ladder attached to the shelving. The shelves were filled with framed photographs, trophies and plaques, and books.

A leather couch and coffee table sat on a Persian rug in the middle of the room, facing a fireplace with a mounted television above the mantle. Behind the seating area, against the length of the back wall, was a bar complete with bottles and glasses on the shelves. There was another raised space just off the side of the bar with two high-backed wing chairs and a table between them. A chess set sat on the table. I looked up and noticed the wooden railing that went around the second floor of the library. There were couches up there too.

"Can I get you a drink?" Evan walked behind the bar and reached for a couple glasses.

"I don't think I can drink anything." My stomach felt tied in knots. I shuffled from one foot to the other, adjusting the bag on my shoulders. I felt out of my league.

"I'm sorry you're in this position."

"It's like being in the twilight zone. Is this what it's like for you?"

Evan shrugged his shoulders. He approached me and held out a glass. I took it from him and took a sip. I felt languid heat pour through me. Scotch. It burned my throat and left a fiery pool of heat in my stomach. This stuff was better than any scotch I'd tasted before. I liked it. Evan took my hand and led me over to sit on the couch.

"You have a beautiful home."

"Thank you."

"I don't understand something." I drank the scotch and allowed more of its warmth to flood through me.

"What?"

"How come you don't have a girlfriend?"

He raised an eyebrow, and I continued. "I mean, you're attractive. You're loaded. You're famous, if the media attention is any indication. Why are you single?"

"Why are you single?" He draped his arms around the back of the couch.

Just like last Saturday in my apartment on the couch, I angled my body to face his. I laughed, feeling some of the tension leave my body. "Because I'm still trying to get my shit together. You're already made. We're not in the same place."

"Looks can be deceiving."

"So, you're not where you want to be?"

"Not quite." He frowned, stared into his glass. "It's tough

to find a girl who doesn't know who I am and what I'm worth. Most women want a relationship with me only because of the size of my... assets."

He smiled, but I sensed the pain in his voice. I thought of the guy I'd seen standing on the sidelines watching last Friday night at Club Yes. He'd been hurt before. "I'm sorry."

He shrugged again. I was beginning to understand that his shrug didn't mean he didn't care. Only perhaps that he did care too much, but that he'd come to terms with the sucky part of his life. I met his honey-brown eyes and felt a desire to make it not suck so much for him. "How do we fix this?"

"It'll past."

"That's not what you and Jake said Saturday night. And after what I experienced at work today, I'm not so sure this is dying down."

"So, what are you saying?"

"Jake's plan."

"What about it?"

"What does it entail?"

"You being my girlfriend."

I felt my heart hiccup at the word. It wouldn't be such a heartache to be his girlfriend. The problem was that the reasons why I didn't want to be in the spotlight still existed. "I have concerns."

He smiled. "Tell me, and I'll see what I can do."

"My job is important to me. My image is important. I can't be made out to be your latest fling."

"That wouldn't be a problem. I don't casually date. You wouldn't be painted in that light."

"I don't want to come across as an opportunist either. I don't want your money."

"You're a nurse—a good one from what I've heard. I doubt anyone would think you're an opportunist."

"What have you heard about me?" Mortification burned my cheeks before I swallowed my pride. My history was a part of me. I'd had no control over it. What mattered now was what I did with my future and the choices I made now.

"Christina Hart. Twenty-four. Deceased mom. Absent father. You grew up in a group home. That's where you met Nadia and Fey. You left at eighteen, enrolled in nursing school. You were hired at Mass Memorial three years ago." He recited the facts of my life like he was reading a bulleted list. There were no emotions on his face.

"You investigated me?"

"Jake did. Saturday. We needed to know who you were before we came to your apartment with the plan."

"The plan to date you."

"Yes. To link our lives together publicly."

"I'm slightly offended that you had me investigated."

"I had to know who I was dealing with."

"Why?"

Evan cupped my face with his hand. He tucked a strand of hair that had escaped my ponytail behind my ear. "Because. You're the first woman I've been attracted to in four years. And I very much want to date you."

I breathed deeply, hoping to still my racing heart. Instead, I inhaled his scent—something spicy and citrusy. It sent a thrill down my spine. "But you don't date."

"I want to date you."

"I don't date."

He nodded. His fingers brushed my cheeks and then curled around the nape of my neck. Moments later, his lips were on mine, crushing, moving, begging me to open for him. I obeyed. He tasted of the expensive scotch we'd just had and of mint. I groaned as sensations exploded in the pit of my stomach. I lifted my free hand to the back of his head and pulled us closer together, deepening the kiss. I could count on one hand the number of guys I'd kissed. I could count on one finger the number of guys who made me feel like this with one kiss. It wasn't the scotch, or the house, or the media frenzy that was doing it. It was Evan.

He lifted his head, and I saw intense desire in his eyes.

"I want you."

Fire and ice tingled up and down my spine causing me to shudder.

"Be my girlfriend."

7
———

Evan

$\mathcal{M}$y phone rang. I pulled away from Christina and reached into my back pocket. I felt a moment of anxiety when I saw my father's face on the screen. I got off the couch and walked over to the bar.

"Hi, Dad."

"Evan, how are you doing, son? Your mom's worried."

He was worried too, but Mom was always a good scapegoat to hang his emotions on.

"I'm good. Lying low."

"This girl. Who is she?"

I glanced at Christina behind me, aware that she could hear my end of the conversation at the least. "A friend."

"Your mom wants to meet her, of course. Come over for dinner tomorrow night. Seven o'clock. Don't be late."

"Sure."

We ended the call, and I pocketed my phone. I wanted another drink, but I wasn't going to have one.

"Hungry?" I asked Christina as I walked out of the library, through the foyer and the open living room to the kitchen.

"I could eat," she said behind me. I glanced over my shoulder to see her studying my home. She walked over to the floor-to-ceiling wall of glass that gave a clear view of my backyard oasis.

I felt a moment of pride at my beautiful house. Then I quickly felt anxiety as I realized I wanted Christina to like it. I needed her seal of approval, and it was so weird because, typically, I didn't need validation from anyone outside of my family.

"This is beautiful," she said, coming into the kitchen. I heard her gasp, turned to see her staring.

"You have a fireplace in your kitchen?"

I glanced at the chest-high fireplace and mantle as I took the lasagna out of the refrigerator and popped it into the oven. It was one of my favorite features about the kitchen. That and the big-ass television above the mantle, of course.

"Makes Sunday breakfast at the island enjoyable." I smiled and hitched my hip against said island.

"Wow." She leaned against the island too, facing me. "You're giving me ideas for my house."

"You're in the market?"

She nodded.

"Fifty thousand could help with the down payment."

Her full, soft lips curved upward, but she said nothing. I already knew what her lips felt like, and damn if I didn't want to kiss them again.

Forty-five minutes later, we were eating warm lasagna at the island in the kitchen with the fire going. I refilled her glass of sparkling water and listened as she ribbed me about how crazy my fans were.

"You should have seen her face when I told her no. One minute, she's staring at me like I'm the best thing since sliced bread, and then she's suddenly about to tear me a new one."

I laughed because it made her laugh, and I loved her laugh.

"So, then Amanda—she's the nurse who was on duty with me—decides she's had enough, and she calls security. Next thing I know, my boss is sending me home for the rest of the week, I'm sure. She said she'll be in touch. But I'm off tomorrow and this weekend. So, she plans to let me know about Monday."

I made a mental note to call Jake about it. I reached for her hand. The frown on her face disappeared. "I wouldn't worry, Christina. You're good at your job. And this will blow over. So, tell me about the fellowship."

"How do you know about the fellowship?"

"I kind of overheard the girls giving you a hard time about it on Friday night."

"Wow!" She chuckled, sipping from her glass of water.

"What can I say? You had my attention the moment you walked through that restaurant."

She met my eyes, held my stare. A shot of desire had me stirring, and I adjusted my butt on the chair. "The fellowship. Spill it."

"It's a fifty-thousand-dollar grant, coincidentally. And an opportunity to study with some of the best doctors and nurses at Mass Memorial. It's also well-known in our field, and it looks great on a resume."

"So, what's stopping you from applying?"

She pushed the food around on her plate.

"When's the deadline?" I tried a different angle.

"Next week, Friday."

"I'll help you."

"Help me?" She snorted. Her eyes were serious though.

"Yes," I said, feeling another emotion other than hot, sexual desire for her. "I'm good at applying for stuff."

"Oh, okay. That makes no sense, Evan."

"I'm serious. Stick around this weekend. We'll work on your application together. I promise to give you a reward when you finish it on Sunday."

"How are you going to help me apply for my fellowship?"

"Well, I've got the space and peace and quiet so you can focus. And I'm good at fetching stuff. You know, water, food, scotch. I'll keep you properly fortified for the task at hand."

"Okay, what kind of reward?"

"Anything you want."

She winkled her nose. I thought fast. "How about premiere tickets to *The Last Dance* for you and the girls."

"Shut up!" She pushed against my arm. I didn't budge, but her warm, soft hand on my arm did wicked things to me and had me imaging her hand brushing against another part of my anatomy.

"I'm serious. Jake reps Michael McKnight. He always gets me tickets."

"You like Michael McKnight?" She raised an eyebrow. A slow smile curved her full lips upward. She was teasing me.

"My sister does."

"You have a sister?"

I nodded, held her surprised stare. "And a brother too. You can meet them when we have dinner with my parents tomorrow night."

"Excuse me?"

"My parents want to meet you. They're a little concerned. It's no big deal."

"You're kidding me, right?" When I said nothing, she continued. "I don't know if that's such a good idea."

"It is. Don't overthink it." I got up, clearing our plates away.

She came to stand next to me as I washed our plates at the sink and set them in the dishrack to dry. "I should leave."

"I made arrangements for you to spend the night."

"Oh, really? Who did you make arrangements with?"

"Nadia."

She burst out laughing, and she moved closer to me, though I don't think she realized it. "That sounds about right."

"She packed a bag for you and gave it to the driver who dropped her home. He should be here soon." I watched her consider my offer. "Come on, what do you say? You could curl up in the library. Watch TV. Drink scotch. Read a book. I'll even light the fireplace for you."

Her eyes lit up. There, I had her.

"I could read." She smiled.

I brushed a lock of hair behind her ear. "Let me take care of you. I promise to walk you to your room tonight and only try to kiss you once."

"I'm afraid once is all it'll take."

I leaned down and brushed my lips against hers. "I'll be a good boy for both of us. Promise."

The peal of the alarm tore us apart. I hit the remote on the wall and the television above the kitchen fireplace came to life in time to show the black Tahoe coming through the front gates. Another image joined the first on the screen when the car turned right into the courtyard and parked outside the garage.

We watched as Tom got out of the car, bringing a black

tote bag with him. Moments later he was at the side door, entering the code.

"Friend of yours?"

"Tom. He handles security for me. He took Nadia home tonight."

Her eyes went wide, and she turned to face Tom as he walked into the kitchen. He set the tote bag down on the island. I got the impression he was happy to complete the task.

I reached out and shook his hand. "How'd it go?"

"Both girls are home safe for the night. No offense Miss Christina, but your friend's a pistol. Gorgeous, but a bit high-strung. Peter's keeping an eye on your place tonight, though I don't doubt your friend could handle anyone who tried something."

"Sorry. Her bite is worse than her sting," Christina offered with a sympathetic smile.

Tom didn't look like he believed it. "Nigel will stay with you two tonight. I'm heading back to the diner to get a cold beer and a huge burger."

"Thanks, Tom. I appreciate you."

"I'll send you my bill." He laughed. "Seriously, though, call me if you need to. And, unless it's urgent, best to stay inside tomorrow and Saturday. Just until some of the heat dies down."

I nodded, grateful that Christina was hearing it from someone other than me.

After Tom left, I grabbed the bag full of Christina's things that he'd left on the table. "Let me show you to your room."

"Okay."

She followed me up the stairs that led from the kitchen to the second floor. I used the opportunity to point out my office, the game room, the media room, the second floor of the library and the three other bedrooms before opening a door and leading her into a secondary master that was directly above my bedroom downstairs. It was corny as hell, but I wanted to stare up at the ceiling knowing she was lying above me.

"It's beautiful."

"Yeah?"

"Yes!" She stared at the four-poster bed and then quickly averted her eyes, walking over to the windows instead and pulling the curtains aside. She had a view of the backyard pool and firepit area.

I was glad I'd let Char take a stab at decorating this room. It was more feminine than any of the others, and I was proud to have Christina stay here.

"Bathroom's this way." I opened the bathroom door and stepped aside for her to enter.

She walked in and gasped. I watched as she walked over to the sunken tub and trailed her fingers along the top of it.

"Can I take a rain check on the library and the fireplace? I think I just want to soak in this tub."

An image of Christina naked and wet flashed across my mind. "Whatever you want."

I watched color bloom on her cheeks. She ducked her head, turning away. I set her bag down, determined to keep the promise I'd made her earlier tonight about being a good boy. "See you tomorrow."

"See you tomorrow."

I was almost out the bedroom door when she stopped me. "Evan." I turned and faced her, still holding onto the door as if it were a buoy in the ocean. "Thank you for everything. For taking care of Nadia and Fey, too. It was thoughtful of you to see that they made it home safely."

"You're welcome."

"Good night."

"Good night, Christina."

I pulled her door shut behind me and headed down the hallway to my office. I shut the door before dialing my financial advisor. It was after eight at night, but Matthew answered on the second ring.

"How can I help?" he asked after we'd exchanged pleasantries.

"I need to fund an investment account for a friend. Fifty thousand to start. I'll send you her information tomorrow. And I want to match whatever Mom donates to Mass Memorial this year."

There was a moment of silence, then Matthew spoke. "Is your friend the mystery woman in the photographs?"

"Yes."

"I can't wait to meet her. I'll bring my camera."

"Ha, ha. How's your wife?" I turned the tables on him. Not too long ago, Matthew had been the talk of the society pages when he'd begun dating his client and had married her shortly after. There'd been a lot of gossip about their marriage being an arrangement. But one only had to see how Matthew adored Caroline August and how she looked at him to know their love was real.

Matthew chuckled. "Your point. I'll put this together first thing tomorrow morning and give you a call with the details."

"Thanks. I appreciate you."

Later, as I lay in bed—alone—and stared at the ceiling above me, I thought of Christina and exactly what I wanted from her. Sex was a given. Yeah, I physically wanted her. She had only to move a certain way and I was rising to the occasion. That in and of itself was amazing and refreshing. After my four-year dry spell, I'd begun to think my dick was broken. And just like that, I felt my cock rise, tenting my pajama bottoms. Christina. She'd brought me back to life, physically.

Had she awoken me emotionally, too? I enjoyed being with her tonight. I hadn't anticipated the companionship I would feel with her. I loved listening to her voice and her laugh. Hearing her talk about her plans to apply for the fellowship and buy a house had made me want to do everything in my power to make her dreams come through.

Shit! I was beginning to care for her.

Unwelcome images from four years ago swarmed my mind. My cock deflated like a punctured football. Bile rose in my throat. I sat up, pushing the covers back, and breathed deeply until the overwhelming emotions of fear and anger dissipated. It was all the reminder I needed, however, of why I couldn't let my guard down. I didn't think Christina was like Isabelle. In fact, the two of them couldn't be more different. But I knew that the circumstances Christina had suddenly found herself in were unlike anything she'd ever experienced.

Sometimes, money and the media made people do stupid things, and they invariably hurt the people they'd never meant to hurt. I'd been burned before, and I still had the fucked-up life to prove it. I wasn't about to make another mistake.

8

Christina

When I woke up on Friday morning, I immediately fired off a text to Nadia and Fey. I'd spoken to Nadia last night during my bath. She'd encouraged me to stay at Evan's, believing that I was better off there than at the condo for the time being. I waited until they both responded that they were okay and that last night had been quiet and uneventful before I changed into leggings and a T-shirt and set out to find Evan.

He stood at the island stove in his kitchen, scrambling eggs. He was wearing sweatpants and a black undershirt that hugged his chest and displayed every well-defined muscle in his torso. He looked up as I walked into the kitchen and took a seat at the island where he was cooking. My God. I could get used to this sight every morning.

"Good morning."

"Good morning. Did you sleep well?"

"I did. I was out like a light after my bath."

He had the fireplace going, and the room felt comfortably warm. Siri had told me it was only sixty degrees outside. Not cold enough for a fire, but Evan did strike me as the type of person who did what he liked when it suited him.

"Want some coffee? Help yourself, Christina. I want you to be comfortable here."

I poured myself a cup of coffee and sat back down at the island. We ate together in companionable silence and I cleaned up after, thinking it was only fair since he'd cooked.

After, we migrated to the library, where we sat on opposite ends of the couch, our feet meeting in the middle. He was reading a hardback book by a transformational guru that I'd heard about but had never found the time to read. I sat with my Kindle in my lap, well on my way through the first act of Charlie McKenzie's latest. It was better than I had hoped, and the wait for its release was proving to be worth it.

Occasionally, I smiled or laughed out loud at something funny the heroine said, and, out of the corner of my eyes, I caught Evan watching me. Soon, he was spending more time looking at me than reading. An hour later, he set his book aside. I looked up and felt my heart slam into my chest. Oh, I knew that look. Answering heat curled in the pit of my stomach. I set my Kindle down on the coffee table.

Evan grasped my ankles with his hands and pulled me farther down the couch, closer to him. Seconds later, his mouth was on mine. I sighed and gave into the desire to lose myself in his kiss. He settled his hands on my waist, held me there beneath him as he totally devoured my mouth. His lips were firm, soft, crushing, worshiping. I was lost in the things he was doing with his mouth. Sensations traveled from my lips to my core. I bent my knee and he settled deeper against me, his hardness pressing into me through our clothes. I lost my breath at the feel of him.

His fingers dipped beneath the waistband of my leggings, trailing along the top of my panties. Anxiety warred with desire. This was heaven, but we were moving too fast. I grabbed his wrist. He stilled. Lifted his head.

We held each other's gaze. I saw his desire for me. I hoped he saw mine. I hoped he saw that I liked his kisses and I wanted so much more. But it was too soon, too fast.

He nodded, pulling back and sitting up.

"So," he said, inhaling deeply, "What are you reading?"

I reached for my Kindle, picking it up. I glanced at his hardback, suddenly embarrassed at my escapism reading choices. "A romance."

"Really? What's it about?" He brushed his palm up my calf.

"A girl who falls for a very handsome, very rich billionaire who she mistakes for a private investigator."

"Huh. Interesting. Who's it by?" Now he was massaging my calf with his big hand in a way that made me want to purr like a very satisfied cat.

"Charlie McKenzie. Have you heard of him?"

His hand stilled as he met my eyes. Then he burst out laughing. He shook his head and stood suddenly, dropping a kiss on my head before straightening. He held out his hand for me to take it. "I have actually. Come on."

"Where are we going?"

He led me through the foyer to the living room, over to the wall of glass. He hit a button on the wall, and I watched as the glass slid back, opening the living room to the backyard and the huge pool that was just a few feet away.

Evan winked at me before running out and cannonballing into the pool. I laughed as he surfaced, shaking his head so that water pitched everywhere. That was one way to do it. The afternoon had warmed up nicely to seventy degrees. I had to wash my hair anyway before dinner tonight, so it didn't matter if it got wet. I looked down at my T-shirt and leggings. I was wearing a sports bra beneath my T-shirt, so I figured I wouldn't cause too much of a distraction if I got the shirt wet.

I didn't even attempt to do a cannonball, having never done one in my life. I suddenly felt self-conscious, and I didn't want to make a fool of myself in front of Evan. I walked around the pool until I got to the steps and climbed down. I braced myself for cold water, but instead it was warm and seemed to part for me to sink into. It was as good as the tub had been last night.

Evan ducked under the water again. I saw his large body cutting through the water toward me. I walked out until the water was up to my chest. He popped up in front of me.

"You're beautiful."

I waited for the feeling of disdain to come that I always felt when people told me that lie, but instead, there was an odd emptiness.

"You are. You do know that right?"

I felt warmth fill that empty place as I stared into his eyes and saw his desire and satisfaction as he looked at me. He thought I was beautiful. It wasn't just a line he was using to get me into his bed. For now, for whatever reason, his words would do.

He cupped my face. "You are beautiful. I'm going to tell you every day—twice a day—until you believe it."

I wrapped my arms around his neck and met his lips for a kiss. The water made me feel light and weightless, and it was easy and effortless holding onto him, pulling him close. His lips moved over mine and it felt like I knew the shape of it, the feel of it by heart. He pulled away, ending the kiss. Then he ducked under the water, diving away.

We were going to end up in bed. Possibly even tonight. Each kiss was a log on the fire of our sexual desire for each other. More to the point, I wanted to make love with Evan. I knew Evan wanted me. I felt the strength of his desire every time he kissed me. He was holding back. Maybe because he was deferring to me. After all, I had stopped him back in the library moments ago.

Now though, I was certain of two things. One, I was meeting his parents tonight. And two, I was making love to Evan, tonight or some night soon. I didn't know where that would leave us. I wasn't sure what the fallout would be for our friendship, but I knew that I wanted my first time to be with Evan.

It had been easy to avoid boys while growing up and bouncing from group home to group home. By the time I'd connected with Nadia and Fey at our last home, I'd been a loner who preferred to keep to myself most of the time. Boys hadn't been on my radar. While Nadia and Fey had gone the college route, I'd focused on nursing. It had kept me tired and exhausted, and again, hooking up with a boyfriend hadn't been my focus.

Now, I was twenty-four and still a virgin. I was a nurse with a steady job. I lived in a good neighborhood near the medical center. I had forged a bond with Nadia and Fey, and they were more like sisters than friends. Yet, I hadn't taken the time to really date. Forget finding a boyfriend. I hadn't been interested. Now, here I was with a rather good candidate.

Evan was a hundred percent boyfriend material. Unless he was a psychotic liar and a sociopath capable of hiding his true nature, he was quite the catch. He'd shown nothing to indicate that he wasn't the type of man I'd imagined. I might be inexperienced, but there was no misunderstanding what his kisses did to me, or the yearning he stirred in me. I might not act on it, but I very much wanted to invite him into my bed and beg him to make love to me.

Perhaps I could tonight, after dinner with his parents. If Evan still wanted me after dinner with his parents. I suspected they had questions about me. I imagined myself in their shoes and knew I would be suspicious as hell about the "mystery woman" who had caused quite a stir in my son's life.

If I were a mother and my son got caught up in a mess like this, I would want to cross-examine the girl too. I would want to make sure she was good enough for him. I lay on my back and floated in the water. I closed my eyes and imagined my son bringing a girl like me home for dinner. Knowing everything I did about myself, would I accept her? Could I blame Evan's parents if they didn't approve of me?

I was making plans to sleep with Evan, but tonight could be my last night with him.

"Hey guys!" I heard the muted voice and stood up. Nigel was standing at the edge of the pool.

"What's up, man?" Evan asked.

"Delivery for Miss Christina. I hung it in the front closet."

"Thanks, I appreciate it. How's it looking out there?"

I swam over to Evan, who was standing at the edge of the pool chatting with Nigel.

"Still a madhouse at the gates, but it's quieted down at the condo. Tom still wants you to stay put."

"Will do. Thank you for bringing it in."

"No problem. Call if you need me."

Nigel smiled at me before putting on his sunglasses and walking away.

"Has he been here the whole time?" I glanced around, wondering if there was anyone else on the property that I had missed.

"I imagine someone relieved him at some point. I'm glad he brought in your surprise."

"My surprise?" I wasn't quite ready to change the topic from Nigel and his access to the house—and whoever else Evan had on his staff who had the ability to come in here at any time. But, like another shiny new object, the delivery overshadowed my other areas of concern. "What is it?"

Evan stared at me for a moment. I thought he wasn't going to answer when he finally spoke. "I got you a dress to wear to dinner tonight. Just in case Nadia didn't pack you one."

"That was thoughtful of you. Thank you."

Evan shrugged his sexy shrug that I loved so much. I smiled, moving closer to him again. "You're a good guy, Evan Kennedy. I'm still trying to figure out why you're single."

"'Cause I hadn't met you yet."

I laughed at the cliche. I'd walked right into that one. "Nothing like a pretend relationship to get the real one going, huh?"

"You're the only one I want to be in a relationship with, pretend or otherwise." He stood in front of me, tall and striking in the sunlight with water dripping from his hair and running down his face. He was dead serious. He meant what he'd said.

"You're the only one I would do this for," I admitted.

"Worried about tonight?"

I nodded.

"Don't be. My parents will love you."

"What if they don't?"

"They will. My sister, too."

My stomach somersaulted at the reminder that his sister was going to be at dinner, too. It was only a little after three in the afternoon, but I headed to the pool steps.

"I want to see my surprise," I called over my shoulder. "And I need to get ready."

"We've still got four hours."

"I need every second."

The cool breeze hit me the moment I stepped out of the water. I shivered, realizing that I didn't have a towel.

"Over there, in the ottoman."

I turned to Evan in time to see him put his hands on the edge of the pool and push himself out of the water. My mouth fell open at the sight of him. His wet clothes clung to his body, outlining every inch of his muscular build. I wanted to run my hands over his torso and back down to his big, muscular thighs. I wanted to touch the package in his pants.

Water dripped off him as he walked over to the ottoman and pulled out two large white towels. He walked toward me, holding one out, never taking his eyes off mine. I saw the slow curving of his lips, the spark of humor and something else in his eyes. Yes, Evan knew what he was doing to me. And, like me, he knew where we were heading.

I took the towel from him and stepped away, wrapping it around me. I went into the house, found the dress hanging in the entryway closet, and escaped to my room.

I took my time showering and washing my hair. Afterward, I dried it with the Dyson blow-dryer I found in the bathroom. It was the model I wanted but had never gotten around to purchasing because it seemed so frivolous to spend all that money on a dryer when my thirty-dollar dryer from Walgreens was still working. Now, as I watched my hair fall like a black cloud, soft and bouncy around my shoulders, I was determined to go straight to the closest beauty supply store at the next opportunity I had and get me one.

I reached for my makeup and decided to go with a natural look. Just a little foundation, a little liner, and some clear lip gloss. I sat in the chair at the vanity and stared at myself in the mirror.

"You've got this."

Liar.

What was I doing? Was I making a mistake? It didn't feel like a mistake. Hanging out with Evan last night and today had been magical. I touched my lips, felt my fingers come away a little sticky. I could still feel Evan on my lips. I could feel his body under my fingertips. It wasn't just about his kisses. I liked the way he treated me, too. He'd cooked us dinner last night and breakfast this morning. He'd sat with me on the couch this morning while I read, content to read too, but mostly to watch me. I loved his companionship. His presence.

I knew what he was doing. He was giving me a taste of what it was like to be in a relationship with him. This was only day two though, and we were on lockdown. Perhaps it would be different once he was able to go out clubbing with his friends again, or when his football season started and he'd have to travel and stay in hotels with his teammates.

I wrinkled my nose at the thought of Evan partying in a hotel room with a bunch of girls and his teammates. The image dissipated as soon as my mind had conjured it up. It was quickly replaced by an image of Evan coming into the hotel room after his game and finding me on the bed, waiting for him, Charlie McKenzie's latest on my Kindle.

"What the actual fuck, Chris?" I said to the girl in the mirror.

I wasn't the type of woman a man came home to. I was the fun girl, with a body made for sex. Evan's path had crossed with mine and was intricately linked now only because of those photographs. Without that twist of circumstance, we most likely would have shared a few more kisses before walking away. He may have asked me for my number, but I might have given him a fake one. Guys like Evan didn't stick around.

He didn't date.

I didn't date.

He didn't do girlfriends.

I'd never contemplated a boyfriend.

But it would be so easy to let Evan be my boyfriend. I was already attracted to him. I liked the way we were together. He was smart and thoughtful. The complete picture.

It was me, not him. I couldn't jeopardize everything I had worked for over a guy who was so out of my league and who was going to leave when all of this blew over.

"Think. Breathe. Get it together!"

I pulled the plastic off the dress Evan had purchased for me. Blue silk caressed my hand as I ran it down the short dress on the hanger. It was long-sleeved, shift-style, and knee-length, with a sweetheart neckline. It was plain but not. I pulled it over my bra and stepped to the mirror. The color of a clear summer sky on a sunny day, the dress highlighted my curves. It was gorgeous.

I walked into the library minutes later. Evan was standing behind the bar, a glass in his hand. His eyes connected with mine across the room.

"You look beautiful."

"Thank you." The fluttering in my stomach had me walking over to the bar and tapping on it.

Evan smiled as he poured me a shot of the scotch I'd grown quite fond of. I took a sip and set the glass down on the bar. Warmth flowed down my throat to my stomach and settled the butterflies there. "What is this scotch?"

"Macallan M Black."

"I'm guessing it's not something I just pick up at Grape, Wine and More, right?"

He laughed as he walked out from behind the bar. "Probably not."

I drained the rest of it and let the warm, sweet, smokey flavor flow its way down to my core. "It's nice."

"It was a gift from my father. He has a bottle over at his house. I'll pour you another glass when we get there."

"I think one glass of this is my limit."

Evan chuckled. "Come on, let's go. You look beautiful. I can't wait for my mom to meet you."

I accepted his hand and let him lead me out to the garage. I expected him to take the Tahoe but was pleasantly surprised when he led me over to the beautifully sculpted two-door sports car. He opened the passenger door for me, and the door swung upward. I laughed at the unexpected but totally cool butterfly door. I noticed the trident on the side of the car's body as I slipped into the seat. Adjusting the hem of my dress, I watched as Evan walked around the front of the car to the driver's seat.

Blue light lit up the low center console and the dashboard as Evan opened his door and slid into his seat next to me. The space seemed to grow smaller, but Evan looked good sitting in the car next to me. I felt a flare of desire and understood why men bought sports cars. It was totally working on me. "I like your car."

He pressed a button on the steering wheel and the engine purred to life before turning into a full-on roar. I laughed. The Maserati logo flashed on the display screen. "I'll let you drive it sometime."

I held my tongue rather than telling him I didn't know how to drive.

I enjoyed the ride as Evan drove out the front gates and down the street. He turned off onto another lane instead of heading down the road to the main gates leading out of the community. I sat back against the soft leather seat and enjoyed my first tour of the beautifully developed community. The houses were big and magnificent. The neighborhood was quiet, even for an early Friday evening. Lampposts rose out of the sidewalks, illuminating the streets and the grassy areas in warm, soft light. Everything about this place was beautiful.

"Tell me about your parents," I said.

"My dad's retired now. Mom's a pediatrician."

"Really?"

"Yeah, she owns a practice with a couple other doctors. She's been cutting back since Dad retired, but she still goes into the office about once or twice a week to see patients."

"And your sister?"

He smiled at me, taking his eyes off the road briefly to meet mine. "She's a writer."

"Really?"

"Yeah. And my older brother, Max, runs the family business. He took it over from Dad."

"Kennedy Enterprises?"

"Yes." He glanced at me again and must have seen my ignorance because he continued. "It's a conglomerate of different companies." He didn't explain more than that and I let it go. I was going to meet them tonight, and it would leave an area for conversation if I legit didn't know much about them. As it was, except for his mom, I wasn't sure that I would have anything remotely in common with them.

After a few moments of driving around McKnight Grove, it dawned on me that Evan's parents also lived here. Evan confirmed my suspicions when he turned onto a private driveway and pulled up to tall, black iron gates. He rolled down his window and punched in a code on the security box. The gates swung open, and he drove up the curving driveway that led to a two-story French Chateau–styled house.

9

Christina

The front door of the house opened just as Evan pulled the car to a stop. An older version of Evan and a young woman about my age stood in the open doorway. I waited until Evan walked around and opened the door for me, holding out a hand to help me out. I was grateful when he held onto my hand as he led me up the front steps.

I stepped to the side as he exchanged a hug with his dad and with his sister. All eyes swung to me.

"You must be Christina. I'm Paul, and this is my daughter, Char."

"Nice to meet you." I shook both their hands.

Paul was as tall and broad-shouldered as Evan, and it was clear that Evan got his build from his dad. Char, on the other hand, was as tall as her brother and father but thinner, with high cheekbones and long black hair that fell in loose waves down her shoulders and back.

"Mom's in the kitchen," Paul said as he closed the door behind us.

The house was like Evan's in that the foyer gave way to a family room across from a kitchen. The kitchen was huge, with floor-to-ceiling white cupboards, granite countertops, and an island with a stove in the middle. A tall woman stood at the stove. She too had long black hair, though hers was pulled back in a high ponytail. Like Char, she had high cheekbones and slanted eyes. While Evan looked like a younger version of his dad, his mom looked like Char's older sister.

Evan walked around the island and gave her a kiss on her cheek before hugging her. "Thanks for cooking, Mom."

"My pleasure. You must be Christina. I'm Brandy." She wiped her hands on a towel before walking over to me. "Thank you for joining us for dinner."

"Thank you for having me."

"What a beautiful dress."

"Thank you!"

She was saying all the right things, but I felt tension coil in my stomach as her eyes took in my appearance from head to toe. She raised an eyebrow before turning to Evan. "I hope you brought your appetite. I made your favorites. Why don't you guys go into the dining room. Char, help me bring the food out."

Moments later, we were all seated at the table, and I was staring at the spread in front of us. A baked turkey sat on a platter in the center of the table, surrounded by sides fit for a state dinner. It looked like something out of a Hallmark Thanksgiving special. Mac and Cheese, green beans, butternut squash, a colorful salad, potatoes with green chives and something else sprinkled on them. Goodness, there was even cranberry sauce.

I realized I was making a mental note of all the foods and then felt foolish for doing so. I couldn't cook. I wouldn't know where to start to prepare these dishes for Evan. And why was I considering making any of this for Evan to begin with? We weren't a real couple. And anyway, I couldn't cook.

I reached for my glass of water, wishing it was something stronger. I caught Char looking at me. She smiled when our eyes connected before reaching for her napkin.

"Sunshine, I paired your meal with the Penfolds Grange Hermitage. I hope it does it justice," Paul said.

Evan's mom laughed. "Is it my meal or is it the company?"

"I promised Christina a glass of your M Black, Dad." Evan nudged me with his elbow as he pretty much told his dad I was a drinker.

"Ah, you know your scotch." Paul looked at me appraisingly.

"No, not really. Only from what Evan keeps at his house." Now, I felt heat rise into my cheeks. Did they know that I was staying at Evan's house? Great, they probably thought I was a freeloading mooch who had moved in with Evan and was drinking my way through his expensive scotch.

A tall man with black hair and a build like Evan's walked into the dining room.

"Evan's taste runs a bit on the common side. You should check out my collection." He smiled as he took the seat opposite mine, next to Char.

"Maximilian!" Brandy frowned at the younger man, who nodded at his dad.

"Really, that's what you're leading with?" Char chuckled.

Evan's hand dropped from the chair to my shoulder. "Christina, meet my idiot older brother, Max."

"The photos don't do you justice."

"Knock it off." Evan leaned forward, tapping his fingers on the table.

"Stop." Paul said the single word. Both men turned to look at their dad. "Did Fisher agree?"

Max shook his head. "I'll fly down there on Monday and meet with her in person. It's not over yet."

"What are we talking about?" Evan asked.

"Your brother's latest acquisition fell through this afternoon." Paul took a sip of his red wine.

"Seems she's not impressed with your wild playboy ways."

Evan scoffed. "Mine or yours?"

"She's referring to four years ago."

Evan went still next to me. A moment later, he reached for his wine glass.

Four years ago? I looked at Evan, prepared to ask him what they were talking about, but his set features and grim face told me now wasn't the time.

Paul spoke softly, "Let's hash this out later. Food's growing cold."

"I agree. Please help yourselves," Brandy said as she reached for one of the sides and scooped food onto her plate.

The atmosphere had shifted with the arrival of Evan's brother, Max. I glanced at him as I reached for the bowl of green beans. His eyes were focused on me, his jaw set in a firm line. My hands were shaking as I picked up the bowl of vegetables.

"So, Christina, what do you do?"

I glanced at Char, grateful for the question. "I'm a nurse at Mass Memorial General Hospital."

"Really? Mom's a pediatrician."

"Yes, Evan mentioned that to me."

"How long have you been a nurse?"

"A little over three years."

"You don't look old enough to be a nurse."

I met Max's eyes across the table. His were cold and flinty. I felt the heat flushing through my body. "I started straight out of high school."

"Did you always want to be a nurse?" Char asked.

"Char, let up a bit." Evan laughed.

"Sorry. Occupational hazard." Char took a bite of her food.

"Oh, that's right. Evan mentioned you're a writer?"

Evan chuckled. "Yeah, Char tell her what you write for a living."

Char met and held my stare. I saw the dare in her eyes. "I write romantic thrillers."

"I love romances! I read them all time," I assured her, feeling an affinity to Char in what felt like hostile territory. "In fact, I'm reading Charlie McKenzie's latest right now."

Brandy stopped eating, her fork halfway to her mouth.

Paul chuckled.

Max muttered, "Right, of course you are."

"Is it good?" Char asked.

"Oh boy, is it good. McKenzie's great. I love everything he writes." I glanced around the table, feeling once more like an outsider. Evan was laughing softly next to me, and Paul and Brandy seemed amused. Max was eating his food now, ignoring us. "I'm an avid reader. You have to tell me what you've written, and I'll check it out on my reader."

"Evan, you're a jackass," Char announced before turning her attention to me again. "You didn't think to tell her?"

I looked around the table. Everyone seemed to be in on the joke. "Tell me what?"

"I write under Mom's maiden name. I'm Charlie McKenzie."

"Char?" I asked.

"Short for Charlotte. Which is often abbreviated as Charlie."

"I see." I felt the heat in my cheeks and knew they were the color of a beetroot. "I always assumed Charlie McKenzie was a man."

"That's the idea."

"Why didn't you tell me?" I turned to Evan, who still had a smile on his face. I didn't think this was funny. He'd let me make a fool of myself.

Evan leaned closer to me, lowering his voice as he spoke in my ear. "I had other things on my mind at the time."

The tips of my ears felt on fire. I took a gulp of water, hoping to get my emotions under control. The anger and embarrassment washed away as a memory of earlier today in the library rolled in. We'd both been distracted on that couch. I wish he'd told me, but I guess I understood why he hadn't.

I ate silently as conversation flowed between Char, Evan, and his parents. Max sat quietly across from me, occasionally grunting a response or answering a question his mom or dad asked. His eyes always seemed to return to mine, however, and I got the feeling that he was sizing me up. I felt like a bug he was watching carefully in case he needed to squash it.

"Thank you. This was lovely," I told Brandy as we wrapped up the meal.

"Thank you, Christina. Why don't we do dessert in the library? You go ahead, and I'll be along shortly."

"I'll help you, Mom." Char said, pushing her chair back and reaching for the plates.

I stood too, gathered mine and Evan's plates, and followed Char into the kitchen.

Brandy looked up as I entered. I caught the flare of surprise in her eyes before she smiled and turned away. "Thank you for helping."

We made quick work of the dirty dishes. Brandy washed and Char and I dried. Char put the dishes away. I had thought we were going to load a dishwasher, but I realized as I watched Char and her mom clean up the dinner table and leave the kitchen spotless that this was a familiar routine for them.

Char kept up a steady stream of conversation the entire time, even asking me questions that drew me into their circle. I caught Brandy looking at me a couple times. I felt her eyes on me at other times. She listened without comment as Char and I spoke, laughing easily with each other. Brandy had an opinion about me, but hell if I knew for sure what it was.

We were each carrying a tray with slices of cheesecake through the front foyer to the library when I heard the rumble of angry voices.

"We can't afford another one of your scandals."

"That isn't what this is. And it's definitely not any of your business."

"Calm down, both of you."

I froze in the library's doorway. Paul stood between Max and Evan. The two men were arms distance away from each other, but they looked like they were about to pounce on each other at any moment. I took a step back and almost bumped into Char.

"We can hear you all the way in the kitchen," Char declared as she stepped around me and walked into the room.

"It's okay. Don't mind them." Brandy smiled as she too walked around me and into the room.

I hesitated still, unsure of my presence. Evan walked over to me and took the tray from me. I followed him into the room. I realized that the library was an almost exact replica of Evan's, except that this one was only one story high.

Paul went to the bar and took a slim, black bottle off the top shelf. He poured a splash of the golden-brown liquid into four glasses. He handed one glass to Brandy and another to me. Evan and Max got the other glasses. Char took the glass of water her father offered her.

"I'm a lightweight." She laughed. "One sip of that and I'll be out for the night."

"To Christina." Paul lifted his glass. Brandy and Evan did, too. I met Max's gaze as he lifted his glass to his lips. I got the feeling he wasn't toasting to my good health.

The scotch was sweet yet smokey on my tongue. It lit a warm fire down to my belly and steadied my frayed nerves.

Evan wrapped his arm around my waist and dropped a kiss on my forehead. I let him lead me over to the couch closest to the fireplace. I remembered what had happened on another couch in a similar library earlier today, and I wished to be back at his house, in his library.

My stomach churned at the thought that Evan and his brother were arguing over the situation that I was very much a part of. I didn't want to be a source of friction between them. Max might be a grade A alpha-hole, but I'd seen enough of him to know he was a serious businessman who didn't enjoy his deal falling through due to our shenanigans.

"I'm sorry. I feel terrible," I whispered to Evan.

"Don't. If anyone should be apologizing it should be Max for being a world-class ass."

"I don't want to cause problems between you and your brother."

"This has nothing to do with you. Trust me."

"Four years ago?" I repeated the phrase I'd heard earlier.

Evan held my gaze and nodded. He swallowed the rest of his drink. I did the same.

"Come on. Let's go home." He took the glass from my hand and set it down on the coffee table.

We said our goodbyes. Char asked me to stop by again. His parents thanked us for coming over as they walked us to the door. Max didn't say a word. There was a history there between Max and Evan. I wanted to know what it was.

When we walked outside, there was a black Tahoe in front of the house, with a man standing next to it.

"George will drive you home," Paul called from the door.

Evan held the back door to the Tahoe open for me and then climbed in behind me. He wrapped his arm around my shoulders, pulling me closer to him. The ride back to the house seemed shorter than the ride to dinner.

"What about your car?" I asked Evan as he unlocked his front door and flipped on a light. A soft glow filled the foyer, illuminating the white tiles.

I turned left into the dimly lit library. The soft lights on the bookshelves and over the bar made the room seem cozier. I loved the library. I realized it was one of my favorite things about Evan's house.

"Someone will bring it back." He sat on the couch, resting his feet on the coffee table. "Come here."

I laughed. This was surreal. Evan's lifestyle was unlike anything I'd experienced before, and he was so nonchalant about it. I wondered if he knew how lucky he was.

I stepped out of my black heels and sat on the couch next to him.

"You look beautiful tonight."

"Thank you for the dress."

"You're welcome." He brushed my hair away from my face. His hand lingered on my shoulders.

"Your parents are lovely. Oh my God! I can't believe your sister is Charlie McKenzie. You should have told me."

Evan chuckled. "Yeah, I'm sorry about that. I wanted to see the look on your face though when you figured it out."

"You're mean."

"Char usually prefers to keep her career a secret. I was surprised she told you. It means she likes you."

"Not so with Max."

"I'm sorry about him. Usually, his bark is worse than his bite."

"Not tonight, though."

"It wasn't you."

I hesitated. I didn't want to overstep. At the same time, I needed to know. "Evan, what happened four years ago?"

Evan sighed. He ran a lock of my hair through his fingers. Then he dropped his hand. He closed his eyes briefly. When he opened them again, I saw determination shining there.

"I was arrested for raping my ex-girlfriend."

10

Evan

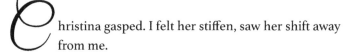hristina gasped. I felt her stiffen, saw her shift away from me.

"I didn't do it."

She exhaled. Nodded.

"It was four years ago. I was a junior at the University of Michigan. I was playing tight end for the team. We were doing good, and I was popular, you know? I was dating a girl I'd met at college. We'd been going out for a couple months, but by that time I think we were both a little over it. One night, after a game, we went to a frat party. I was exhausted. I wasn't up for it."

I could hear the music from the party. I could feel the heat of the house and the irritation of being somewhere I didn't want to be. Sweat beaded on my upper lip. I focused on Christina. Her face, pale and grim, pulled me into the present.

"Forty minutes at that party and I'd had enough. I

wanted to leave. She wanted to stay. She'd already been drinking, and she was having a good time. We ended up arguing about it. She broke up with me. I lost my temper. I was so angry with her that I left her there."

Christina shook her head. I saw the horror on her face. I closed my eyes and continued. I had to be honest with her. She needed to know.

"Six hours later, the police were knocking on my door. One of her friends had found her passed out in the back-yard and called an ambulance. She'd been raped. They didn't believe me when I said it wasn't me because she had given my name along with two other guys when she'd come to."

"Oh no." Christina reached for my hand, held it tightly.

"I don't know why she did it. If she was angry with me and thought to get back at me. Or if she was just confused. Four days later, she told the police I'd had nothing to do with it. She told them the truth—that we'd fought and broken up and I'd left her there. She'd hooked up with one of my teammates. She started feeling sick. He took her upstairs to his room to sleep it off. Later, he and his friend went back to the room and assaulted her. The police suspected he'd slipped sleeping pills into her drink so she'd pass out.

"It took two weeks for the results from the rape kit to come back, and that was with my father's lawyers doing a lot of pushing. By then, it was about damage control for me, for my family's business. The media was relentless, digging up every party I'd attended, questioning every girl I'd dated. That's why Dad hired Jake. I was going to switch colleges, but then Jake had the idea for me to skip my senior year altogether and go straight to the NFL. I didn't think any team would want me with the media circus, but I got drafted to the Houston Texans. Which was fine with me. It meant I could come home. Put it behind me."

"Have you?" Her voice was a caress in the quiet library. She squeezed my hands. I saw the tears in her eyes.

"Mostly I have. Those first three days were a nightmare. First the questioning at the station. It didn't matter how many times I said I didn't do it. The police didn't believe me. It was hours before they let me call my dad. That was tough, explaining to Dad that I was being held at the police station on suspicion of rape."

Now, I remembered my dad's silence on the other end of the phone. Then his calm yet firm voice telling me to hold on, he was on the way.

"The two weeks of being under suspicion were hell. But I think it was worse for my mom and dad. And Char, too. She didn't leave the house for six weeks straight because when she did, the media hounded her. Max saw what it did to them and, even though he knows I didn't do it and it wasn't my fault, he still blames me for putting them through that ordeal."

"That's not fair. No one could have imagined that would happen."

"I wish I hadn't left her there."

"Would she have gone with you?" Christina cupped my cheek. Her palm felt soft on my face.

"Four years later and I know the answer to that question is still no. We were toxic together that night. Even if I hadn't gone to the party with her, I think she would have still gone by herself. But it's easy to wish I'd done something different that night."

"What happened to her?"

"Last I heard, she was a lawyer working in New York."

"And the guys who raped her?"

"In jail."

Christina nodded, releasing a deep sigh. She wrapped her soft arms around me and rested her head on my shoulders. I felt the tension, the anger, the pain, and the heartache recede to a pinpoint before flickering out like a dying candle. Peace flowed through me for the first time in days. I focused on the woman in my arms now and breathed in her vanilla and coconut scent.

"I'm so very sorry you had to go through that." Her voice rang with sincerity.

Relief pushed the pain away. Christina knew, and she wasn't running. It hadn't changed the way she saw me. She didn't think less of me.

"That's why last Friday shook me up so much. I've stayed out of the media since, and Jake and I do a good job of controlling my image."

"That's why you don't date?"

"That's more a matter of preference. There hasn't been anyone I've wanted to date."

"In four years?"

I shrugged, and she grinned. "My career and my side businesses have kept me preoccupied."

"So, you haven't had a girlfriend since?"

"I pretty much kept my head down and played football. Until last Friday night, when I looked up and saw you walking through that restaurant. So damn sexy." Color bloomed like apples on her cheeks. "I wanted you so badly. You took my breath away."

She lifted her mouth to mine, and I kissed her. Pleasure lit like dynamite and exploded inside of me, like fireworks in the sky on the Fourth of July. She tasted fruity yet smokey. The Macallan was delicious on her tongue.

I yearned to make love to Christina. I wanted nothing

more than to lose myself in her, here, right now in the library, but it was too soon. What if sex ruined what we had going on? I didn't want her to hate me. And I didn't want to hate me if this all turned out to be a huge mistake and I'd dived headfirst over another cliff. I didn't want to make a mistake with Christina that would haunt me for years the way my mistakes with Isabelle did.

I wanted more than a hookup with a girl I'd met at a club on a Friday night. I wanted to make love to Christina. I needed her to want the same thing. I needed it to mean more to Christina than the attention, the house, the cars, the expensive lifestyle. I needed more. "I want us to be sure before we take this next step. I don't want to rush you."

Her eyes focused on mine. She breathed in deeply. "I don't want to be rushed either."

"Please stay. Spend tomorrow with me. We can hang out here together. Get to know each other better. I did promise to help you with your fellowship application. What do you say?"

She was thinking about it. I saw the desire in her eyes warring with the worry and concern. Finally, she nodded. "Okay. I'll stay."

I almost fist pumped the air. I was happy in a way that I hadn't felt in a long while. Carefree, too, as if I had nothing to think about. No worry in the world. It was exhilarating.

"I'm going to walk you to your bedroom now. And I'm only going to kiss you once." I got off the couch, pulling her to her feet too.

She scrunched up her nose. She wasn't happy about that. I loved that I knew her tells and I could read her so well. I hadn't felt this close to another woman—ever. Not even my ex-girlfriend.

Christina could be the one who made me want to dive

back into an exclusive relationship. It wasn't just about her physical beauty. I loved how she thought, how she saw the world. I loved how kind and thoughtful she was. Her determination to make a better life for herself was refreshing. As was the way she didn't let her challenging childhood affect her now.

I walked Christina to her bedroom door and kissed her goodnight. I did a great job of walking away rather than asking if I could stay. I already cared for her. I wanted more time with her. I needed to know if this was the real deal or just sparks flying, caused by incredible chemistry. I'd had that groundless relationship before. It wasn't anything I could ever be attracted to again. I needed to know what this was between Christina and me. I already suspected. But I needed to know for sure.

11

—————

Evan

Christina and I spent the weekend together at my house. Being with her was effortless, so easy, it made the thought of being apart from her incomprehensible. We cooked our meals together. We swam together in the pool. We cuddled in the theater, making out more than watching the movie. I taught her how to play chess on Sunday, and when she'd had enough, we made out some more on the couch in the library. And each time I was kissing her, it felt righter than anything else had felt in a long time.

We were just sitting down to dinner when I heard the alarm peal. I flipped on the television in the kitchen in time to see Jake's Range Rover pulling through the gates and around to the courtyard. Moments later, he was walking into the kitchen.

"I'm sorry to interrupt." Jake clasped me on the shoulder before reaching out to shake hands with Christina.

"No problem. Have you eaten?" I reached for a third plate. Jake often got lost in work stuff and forgot to eat.

"Not yet, but I don't want to take up too much of your time. I stopped over to discuss tomorrow and what you can expect from this week."

Christina put her fork down and set her napkin next to her plate.

"Let's move to the table." I handed Jake his plate of lasagna and picked up mine and Christina's. She followed behind me, bringing the napkin and silverware.

When we were all seated, Jake continued. "Christina, you've got a few photographers parked in front of your apartment building. They may follow you, take your pictures as you come and go. It's a good idea to have Nigel continue to drive you around. Just for safety."

She didn't like that one bit. I spoke before she could voice her objection. "Do it for a couple of days, just so we can be sure you're safe."

"What about when I'm at work? Is Nigel going to follow me around the hospital as well?"

"No, not unless it proves to be necessary." Jake continued, "I've a meeting with the chief of staff and your supervisor tomorrow morning. Try not to worry, I'm smoothing it out."

Christina looked from Jake to me. I smiled reassuringly, hoping she would see that she didn't need to worry. I wasn't going to stand by while she lost her job. At the same time, I wasn't going to leave her out on the hook for the media to have a field day with her. If Nigel needed to stay glued to her side to keep her safe, that was the way it was going to be.

"Now, about you two." Jake looked at me. I met his eyes and waited. "I'd like to arrange for some photographs of the two of you together to start making the rounds. Nothing major, just you two out on a dinner date, or running at the park down the street together. It would help to solidify the idea that you're in a normal relationship and that there's no story here."

"Wouldn't that put a bigger target on my back?" Christina asked.

"People are already curious about you, Christina. This gives them a little more access, but the key is that we control the story. People love a romance. Everyone roots for love."

"But we're not in love," Christina said softly.

A fierce objection flared to life. I ignored the urge to protest and kept my mouth shut.

Jake continued. "A romance helps Evan more than a one-night hookup."

Christina's cheeks turned red, and I saw red. "That's not what's happening here, Jake."

Jake looked back and forth between the two of us. He nodded. "True, and we need to make sure the media knows that. Neither of you can afford a tarnished reputation right now. Evan, let's not forget that your deal with MacMillan Brothers isn't finalized yet. Christina, your hospital has a staunch reputation for being one of the most elite teaching hospitals in the country. Both organizations have high moral standards. They're not going to take kindly to any kind of negative attention."

I met Christina's gaze across the table and held it. I could see the questions in her eyes. I tried to tell her I had her back. "Would it be such a hardship to let me take you out to dinner at Bartholomew's on the Bayou?"

She lifted an eyebrow. "Bartholomew's?"

I nodded.

"Okay," she said, smiling.

"Jake," I said, turning to my friend. "You've got a deal. Please, don't make Christina regret it."

Jake smiled and winked at Christina. Then, reaching for his fork, he took a bite of the lasagna. "This is great. Did you make this?"

I shook my head and took a bite. "Mom brought it over earlier this week. There's another one in the freezer. You can take it with you."

"Thank George," Jake said.

I smiled and looked over at Christina. She was eating too, though she seemed to be a million miles away. I knew she was worried about the plan, but I felt a little hurt at the wall that suddenly seemed to separate us. I reached across the table and took her hand. "Hey, stop worrying."

Christina grasped my hand, but then she pulled away and set her fork down. "I should go back to my apartment tonight. Get ready for tomorrow."

I could feel her retreating from me. "Okay. I'll take you."

"Why don't I? It's on my way and I don't mind."

My stomach clenched at the thought of Jake and Christina alone in his car. I imagined him holding her hand to help her out of his Range Rover and walking her to her front door. "I got it."

"Evan, let's avoid the media frenzy of you pulling up in front of Christina's apartment tonight. I'll do it."

I frowned at him. When exactly was the media frenzy acceptable? Only when he was orchestrating it? Wouldn't I be taking Christina home after one of the dates he had planned for us, and therefore causing a media frenzy?

"It's okay. Jake can take me." Christina pushed her chair back.

Well. Shit. I looked at her as she gathered up our empty plates, but she didn't meet my eyes. She was trying to get away from me. I felt the hardness in my gut. I kept my mouth shut and watched her exit the room.

I wanted to follow her. I wanted to wrap my arms around her and hold her until she met my eyes. I wanted to kiss her until she was begging me for more. But I folded my arms and remained at the table.

"She's nervous about tomorrow," Jake said in way of an explanation.

I felt pain in my jaw and realized I was clenching my teeth. Forcing myself to breathe deeply, I focused on the man sitting across from me. "I don't need you to explain Christina to me."

Jake's eyebrows drew together. He studied me in silence for what seemed an eternity before he exhaled his breath on a rush. "Damn, Evan." He sounded hoarse, his voice almost gravelly. He rose from the table and walked out into the foyer.

I went upstairs to my office and turned on the light. The lamps in the corner of the room and on my desk cast a soft glow around the room. I saw the two chairs we'd pulled in front of my computer as we worked together. My computer screen was black now. I walked to the printer and picked up the fellowship application we'd completed and printed off earlier today. All that was left to do was for her to sign it and turn it in.

Jake and Christina were standing by the side door to the courtyard when I came down the stairs. Jake was already holding her weekend bag. He said his goodbyes, promising to call me.

I nodded, not really wanting to talk to Jake right now. I reached for Christina's hand and felt relief when she wrapped her fingers around mine. She seemed small standing in front of me in leggings and a T-shirt. I remembered how good she'd looked on Friday in identical clothes but soaking wet from us romping in the pool. She'd been carefree and happy then. Tonight, she seemed unsure. A little afraid.

"I promise you, it's going to be alright."

She looked at me with unreadable eyes, masking her thoughts. "Thank you, Evan. I enjoyed our time together."

"That sounds like a goodbye."

"It is. But, only for now. Right?"

"Absolutely! We're having dinner tomorrow night, right?"

"Can't wait."

"It'll be a celebration as well, for turning this in." She looked down at the application I held out to her. She laughed hesitantly and reached for it. I held it out of her reach. "Promise me, you'll turn it in tomorrow."

She snatched it from me. "Of course I'm turning it in tomorrow."

We laughed together, and it felt like we were back to the two people who'd been great companions all weekend.

"What time do you want Nigel to pick you up tomorrow morning?"

I saw the hesitation again. I shook my head before she could protest. She smiled. "Six thirty is fine."

"He'll be there."

"Thank you. I appreciate everything you and Jake are doing."

"It's Jake's job. But it's my pleasure."

She smiled and reached for me. I let her pull my face down to meet her lips and felt the heat of our kiss flow through my body to all the right places.

"Goodbye, Evan."

"Goodbye, Christina."

I walked her to Jake's Range Rover and tried not to glare at him as he stood there holding the passenger door open for her. I would have preferred if she'd sat in the back. God damn it! I was losing my mind.

I watched the icy blue Range Rover drive out of my courtyard. I found myself wondering if she wished it was me driving her home tonight instead of Jake. I turned and walked back into the house. The house seemed silent and huge now. I'd never noticed what a big-ass house I had. And why did I have such a goddamned big house? It had seemed like a good idea to snatch up this lot when the McKnight Grove community was being developed. Especially since my dad had moved on a property not too far away. But now I wondered just what I'd been thinking. I'd never noticed before how much space I had.

I ignored the mess of dishes in the kitchen sink as I walked by. I opened the door down the hall and flipped the lights on in the gym. I eyed the punching bag, feeling like I could go a round. In the end, I settled for a mind-numbing run on the treadmill.. It took me ten minutes to reach that space where the thoughts stopped running through my mind and everything—and everyone—ceased to exist.

12

Christina

"*E*van cares for you."

I tore my eyes away from the buildings rushing by outside my window and looked at Jake. His hands were on the steering wheel, and he was staring straight ahead at the road in front of us.

I ran my sweaty palms down and up again on my cotton-clad thighs. It felt like my insides were vibrating at his words. I swallowed deeply and felt my heartbeat in my throat. "He's a good man."

"He is. One who can easily be taken advantage of."

I stilled as a sudden heaviness descended on me, dragging me down in my seat. It left me numb inside. I didn't respond.

Jake continued, "This is an unusual situation that presents a unique opportunity for you."

"What the hell are you trying to say?"

"Evan has your best interest at heart. I want to make sure you've got his."

I did. Of course I did. But I felt my stubbornness rising, fueled by my hurt and my offended pride. After a moment of silence, Jake looked across at me and held my eyes for one second, two, three. I looked away first, watching the road, because damn it, one of us needed to.

We drove the remaining five minutes in silence. Jake pulled into the parking garage and drove up to the second level. He parked the car. I reached for the door handle, but his words stopped me.

"Promise me one thing."

I didn't want to promise him a damn thing. But, I stilled, waiting, my hand on the door.

"When the media comes to you to buy your story, call me."

The fact that he'd said when, not if, made my heart race like a horse at the Kentucky Derby. I took a deep breath, exhaled. I let go of the door and turned to face him, needing him to see me when I said it. "I would never do anything to hurt Evan."

"You say that now, but someone like you could benefit from the money."

"Someone like me?"

He looked away. When he met my eyes again, he leaned forward, exhaling deeply. "Look, I'm not trying to be an asshole, okay? It's my job to look out for Evan. Hell, he's like a brother to me. And he's a good guy. I would look out for him even if he didn't pay me a shitload of money to do it. I'm asking you to think before you do anything that would jeopardize him."

I felt my anger deflate like a popped balloon. Jake cared deeply for Evan, and he was doing his job. He wasn't the only one who would think I was attracted to Evan because of his money and his famous career. I was a nurse, and though I made good money, it wasn't billionaire money. No way like what Evan had. Jake wouldn't be the only one to judge me. I would need thick skin if I was to make this work.

Make what work? I laughed out loud in the car and stopped abruptly because my laugh vibrated and sounded hollow and sad even to my ears.

All men left, and Evan wasn't going to be any different, no matter how much of a good guy he was. We enjoyed each other, but sooner or later something or someone would come along who would be more up to his speed. "I promise, Jake. You don't have to worry about it."

He frowned. Seemed about to say something, but hell if I hadn't had enough. I opened my car door and slammed it shut behind me. I heard him get out on his side and walk around to the trunk for my bag. I held out my hand to take it from him, but he shook his head. "I'm walking you to your front door. Evan would kill me if I left you here in the parking garage.

It was true, so I didn't give him a hard time. Instead, I pulled my phone out of the side pocket of my leggings and quickly tapped on Nadia and Fey's group chat.

"Incoming." I typed the one-word warning and slipped the phone back into my pocket.

Jake and I rode the elevator up to my floor in silence. What else was there to say? We'd reached an understanding of where we both stood. Or at least, I hoped he knew where I stood. I wasn't here to take advantage of Evan. And Evan didn't need protecting from me. If anything, I needed protection from the potent way Evan made me feel.

I had never cared for a man like this before. I used to think that I cared for my father, but he'd walked out on my mom and me years ago and, with each year that he hadn't returned, whatever feelings I'd had for him had simply dried up until there was nothing left. Except for Nadia and Fey, there wasn't anyone that I cared about.

Now, what I felt for Evan terrified me and arrested me. It fascinated me, and it tormented me. If my relationship with Evan was only for a moment, how would I handle my feelings when it was over?

I held out my hand to take my bag again, but Jake just nodded at my front door. I rolled my eyes and pulled my keys out of my pocket. I unlocked the door and stepped into my apartment. Turning around, I faced him.

"There, satisfied now? I'm safe and sound, and you can tell Evan you did a good job."

His lips twitched, and he was about to make a comment when he lifted his eyes suddenly and inhaled sharply. He stood still, whatever he was about to say lost as he stared over my shoulder. I turned to see Nadia standing in the hallway, a dark frown on her face.

"I texted you."

"My phone's in my bedroom." She held up her cup of coffee.

I saw the flush creep into her cheeks. She was wearing a tank top and boy shorts and not much else. We'd caught her unprepared from the looks of it.

"Thank you for the ride, Jake. Nice chat." I grabbed the bag from his hand and shut the door in his face. I leaned against the door and mentally prepared myself for the conversation I knew I couldn't escape having with Nadia.

"I wasn't sure you would come home tonight."

"Work tomorrow. Sorry I ditched you guys all weekend."

"It's okay. Was probably for the best. The media camp

disbanded this morning once they realized you weren't here."

I sighed, adjusted the bag in my hand. "Just say it, Nadia."

"Do you know what you're doing?"

"Yes. I do."

"You stand to lose a lot. A hell of a lot more than Evan Kennedy. I've never seen you like this over a guy. Look, I just want to make sure you know what you're doing. I don't want to see you get hurt."

Not for the first time tonight, I felt irritation bloom. "What makes you think Evan's going to hurt me?"

"Evan seems like a nice guy, and I don't think he will hurt you intentionally. But, Chris, I'm more concerned with you and how you're handling this. You've not been in a relationship before." Nadia paused. She looked down at the cup in her hand. I could see the wheels turning in her mind. When she looked at me again, there were tears in her eyes. "Whatever you need. I'm here for you."

Shit. Now she'd made me cry. "Next time, sweetie, lead with that." She laughed as we hugged in the hallway. I could hear her heart racing against my ears. "Thank you for being my friend."

"Always."

"And my sister."

"Forever."

I pulled away from her and walked into my bedroom, shutting the door behind me. I slid down against the door until I was sitting on the floor. I drew my knees to my chest and wondered just what in the world I'd gotten myself into.

13

Christina

I watched the photographers outside of the car, wondering how so many of them had known that Evan and I were going to be at Bartholomew's on the Bayou. Had Jake put out some type of bulletin blast? The exclusive, upscale restaurant was a favorite of Evan's, but it was my first time coming here. Bartholomew's required a reservation, and dishes were in the hundreds a plate. My friends and I didn't hang out here. Not even on special occasions.

Nigel pulled the Tahoe to a stop and walked around to my side of the door. He opened it and helped me out of the SUV. Evan slid across the seat and exited on my side as well. The night exploded to life with the sound of camera clicks and flashing lights. The three of us walked into the restaurant together. The photographers were busy snapping pictures, but I noticed that they didn't scream questions at us, nor did they try to approach. All in all, it wasn't too unpleasant an experience.

Evan released a sigh in obvious relief as we stepped through the front door. A hostess greeted us and led us to the back of the restaurant, where there was a quiet alcove with a table set for two. Evan held the seat out for me before walking around to his chair. Nigel, I noticed, had been seated at a table a few feet away from us.

"Wow. This is nice." I smiled at Evan.

He looked around, nodded, took a sip of his water, and smiled at me. He was nervous. We'd agreed to Jake's idea, but it hadn't been Evan's first choice.

"Honestly," he said, leaning across the table and reaching out his hand to take mine, "I'd rather be in my kitchen cooking for you."

I smiled at the thought, then wondered if it was because he would rather not be seen in public with anyone—lest the media went back to that time four years ago—or if it was just that he didn't want to be seen in public with me. I pulled my hand away and reached for my menu.

"You look beautiful."

I dropped my menu and stared at Evan. "Thank you." Handsome did not begin to describe him. I didn't tell him so though. He'd found time to get a haircut sometime this week, and I missed the piece of his unruly hair that use to fall over his forehead.

"So, what's good to eat here?" I asked.

"Everything. The chef's pretty good. Hopefully she's available later so you can meet her."

"You know the chef?" I ignored the sudden burning feeling in my chest. I took a sip from my water glass and waited for his answer.

Evan smiled, and I couldn't help focusing on his mouth. I knew how it felt on mine. I missed that feeling.

"Max financed her first restaurant. I've met her a couple

times."

"Ah." The mention of his brother caused a small chill to run down my spine. I remembered Max's mysterious dark-brown eyes studying me on Friday night. "So, your family business? Is that what it is? Financing restaurants and stuff?" I remembered Max had been upset about some deal.

"Amongst other things. Kennedy Enterprises has a stake in a little of everything. It's been in our family for three generations now. My grandfather on my father's side started it and passed it on to my father, and he passed it to Max."

"Not you?"

"No, not me." He smiled, indicating that there were no hard feelings there. "I love football, and lucky for Dad and me, Max loves K.E. He lives and breathes the company. There was never any question about him taking over once Dad retired. I do sit on the board, and I get to vote on some key issues every once in a blue moon, but Max runs a tight ship, and he runs it to his liking."

I raised an eyebrow at the comment but remained silent. I could see Max Kennedy running the business himself and calling all the shots. Evan's brother was intimidating across the dinner table. I didn't want to see him in action trying to close a deal.

"What about you? Did you always want to be a nurse?"

The waiter appeared at that time. Evan and I gave our orders, and Evan asked for a specific bottle of wine to be brought over as well.

"I think you'll like it," he teased me as the waiter walked away.

"I trust your judgment. But now I'm curious—how do you know so much about alcohol? Scotch, wine. Are you well versed in all forms, or are those two the extent of your knowledge?"

Evan laughed, shook his head. "K.E. owns a vineyard in California. As for the scotch, I learned that from my dad. He's serious about his whiskey."

I laughed. It seemed that Evan and his father were both connoisseurs of fine liquor. And the more expensive the bottle the more they liked it. But I wasn't going to fault them, since the M Black I'd had last week had tasted better than any glass I'd had at a club.

"How's Char? I can't believe she's your sister. I love her books."

"She's good. She enjoyed meeting you, and she wants us to get together again. I think she wants to pick your head about being a nurse."

"I doubt it. Your mom's a physician. I doubt Char needs any info from me."

Evan shrugged. "I wouldn't be so quick to dismiss your nursing skills. Besides, Char's curious about most everyone, and most everyone ends up in one of her books at one time or another."

"Even you?"

"Everyone except family. Char respects our privacy. Now, enough about me. I feel like we're always talking about me."

The waiter appeared with the bottle. I watched as he uncorked it and poured a bit for Evan and me. I followed Evan's actions, taking a small sip of the wine. Flavor burst to life on my tongue. "Wow."

"Yeah?" Evan smiled.

"Yes! I love it."

"We'll keep the bottle." Evan nodded to the waiter.

I laughed as he filled my glass. "So, is this one of your labels?"

"It is."

I looked at the label. *Napa Valley McKenzie Estates.* There was a picture of rolling hills with a house on top of it on the bottle. "And, of course, now I recognize the name McKenzie."

Evan nodded. "My dad renamed the vineyard in honor of my mom's dad. His way of thanking him for raising my mom all by himself. My grandmother passed away when Mom was five."

"Is he still alive? Your grandfather?"

"No, he passed away a couple years ago."

"I'm sorry." I offered my condolences and fell silent. Hearing about Brandy's childhood made me think about my own father and the different choice he'd made.

Evan reached across the table and took my hand. "I've made you sad."

I smiled, squeezed his hand. Evan was so sensitive to those around him. I'd seen him hyperaware of his mom, his sister, even Nadia and Fey. But he was especially attuned to my emotions, my thoughts, and my reactions. He was great at reading me.

"I was thinking about my mom. She passed away when I was eight. I didn't have any other family." I saw sympathy fill his eyes. "Until I met Nadia and Fey, that is. They're like my blood sisters. I'm never lonely thanks to them."

The meal arrived, halting the conversation. We spent the next five minutes raving over how delicious each of our meals tasted. Evan let me dip my fork in his risotto and take a bite of it. It was to die for. I let him have a bite of my creamed spinach.

"This is sooo good. It's decadent."

"Wait until you taste the crème brûlée. It's made in heaven."

The waitstaff had just finished clearing away our dinner plates, and the waiter was walking away to get our dessert, when I suddenly remembered one of the purposes for tonight's date. "Should we wait for the photographer to take the pictures?"

Evan shrugged. "Jake's got his plan, and I've got mine."

"Ohhkay."

"And I'm working my plan right now."

I laughed out loud and then took a sip of the wine.

"Tell me, did you always want to be a nurse?"

I thought about it for a moment. Evan was waiting for an honest answer, and I supposed I owed him the same honesty he'd given me when he'd shared his painful past with me. "No. I didn't." I took a sip of the wine and continued. "I was always helping to clean up cuts and scrapes at most of the group homes I lived at though. So after high school, when I needed to pick something to do, nursing stood out as an option. I didn't really want to do the four-year college route. I figured nursing was a good choice for me. It offers great job security, it pays well, and I'm good at it."

"How long were you in foster care?"

"Ten years."

I saw his eyebrows lift in surprise. Heard his swift inhale.

"That's how I met Nadia and Fey. At the last home I stayed at. We gravitated toward each other. We were all the same age, and our birthdays were all in August. We aged out at the same time. We got along so well, it just made sense to stick together."

"I'm sorry about your mom. But where was your dad?"

I looked around the quiet alcove. There were tall palm trees spread around the corners of the room. Water poured out of a shelf in the back wall and fell over the shelf into a basin at the bottom. I realized the place felt like a Caribbean Island or a rainforest. It was peaceful, relaxing. I liked it.

"He left when I was five."

"Left?" Evan asked.

"Walked out. Disappeared. I haven't seen him since."

Evan's hands settled on mine again. "It's his loss."

"You're so sweet. Why are you single again?"

"I'm not. I'm dating this hot nurse. Haven't you heard?"

I laughed and decided the wine was going straight to my head. As if on cue, the waiter appeared with our desserts. A woman who was about five foot six with a cream and coffee complexion and dressed in a white chef's jacket followed closely behind.

"Evie!" Evan stood and hugged her.

"I heard I had a Kennedy in the house. It's good to see you, Evan. How are you?"

"Never been better. This is Christina."

"Nice to meet you." Evie shook my hand, with the hint of a smile on her lips. What were the chances she hadn't seen any of the publicity around Evan's and my relationship? I was guessing zero to none.

I listened as Evie and Evan chatted about this restaurant and the second location she and Max were working on. It was scheduled to open in December. When she smiled at me and invited me to come to the soft opening, I smiled back and said I would, even though I doubted Evan and I would still be together eight months from now.

Our relationship was a media ruse. We were just having fun, and I didn't expect it to last. Evan was a great guy. I knew he enjoyed our time together, and I hoped he would want to remain friends. I had never had a long-term relationship with a man before. All my experience pointed to the fact that men left. There was always something newer and shinier around the corner. Evan had gone four years without dating anyone. Once this situation was behind him, it would be easy for him to fall back into that pattern. A long-term girlfriend wasn't something he was looking for. His history indicated that.

"She seems nice," I said to Evan after Evie had left.

"She is. Temperamental as fuck though. Max is terrified of her."

"No!" I laughed out loud, glancing at Evie, who was across the room chatting with a couple at another table.

"Yep. Gives her whatever she wants. He says it's only wise since she has the power to poison him at any time and make him enjoy it."

I laughed. So, Max had a sense of humor. But he was right—I would eat anything Evie set in front of me. Her cooking was that good. Case in point, this crème brûlée, which was currently melting on my tongue.

"You make me want to kiss you when you lick your lips like that."

His words sent a shiver racing up my spine. The hairs on my arms stood up, and I found myself wanting to lean across the table and press my mouth against his. I suddenly felt light-headed, but I didn't think it was the wine. No, this feeling of desire was all caused by Evan. The thought of kissing him again, after two days of not having his kisses, made me lean toward him, lips parting.

"Come home with me tonight," he whispered.

I crossed my legs and put my fork down on my plate. I longed to run my fingers through his hair. Or cup his high cheekbones with my palm. More than anything, I wanted to press my body against the full length of his and lose myself in his kiss. "We should go dancing!"

"Dancing?"

"Yeah, like we did at Club Yes."

He scrunched up his nose and looked away. I burst into

laughter and pointed at him accusingly. "You just made my face."

"What?"

"That face you just made. That's my face."

Evan laughed.

"So, it's a no to Club Yes?"

"A hard no. But I know a private room with a bar and a great sound system. It's got a cozy fireplace I can light for you. I've heard it's one of your favorite places, too."

I was so tempted to go back to Evan's place. But, if I did, I knew we would make love. I wanted to, so badly. But I was terrified. What if he never called again? What if he disappeared like the wind after tonight and I never saw him again? I wasn't ready to say goodbye to him yet. I wasn't ready for this to end. Not yet.

Evan placed his hand on top of mine. "Okay. No pressure. I'll take you home."

He signaled for the waiter and handed him his black credit card.

"Are you working tomorrow?"

I nodded.

"Can I take you to dinner and a movie tomorrow night?"

"You don't have to do that," I protested.

"Yes, I do. Wait!" He held up his palm. "Let me clarify that. I want to spend more time with you, and I want to kiss you. But I wouldn't ask you to spend the night with me. It'll totally be your move."

That might prove to be as big a problem as if he was asking me to sleep with him. I wanted him on a purely basic level that had nothing to do with rational thought or fear of him leaving me. "Okay, deal."

Later that night, Evan held my hand as we rode the elevator up to my apartment in silence. He walked me to my door. I put my key in the lock and turned it, opening the door slightly. I stopped and faced him. I needed to know. "Are you mad?"

"That I'm not taking you home tonight?" he asked, cupping my cheeks in his large hands. "I'd be lying if I said I wasn't disappointed. I want to make love to you, Christina. But you're worth the wait."

I nodded. "Okay." His words had warmth flowing all the way through my body to my core. I held onto the front of his shirt and pulled him down toward me.

Our lips touched softly at first, exploring, then with all the passion and remembering from last weekend. When we pulled away moments later, we were both breathing a little harder and clinging to each other for sweet life.

"You're dynamite, Christina."

"You're the match, Evan."

He closed his eyes, leaned his forehead against mine, and pressed his lips to mine again.

"Go on in before I beg to follow you to your room."

I laughed. "Good night."

"Bye, Christina."

I closed the door and leaned against it, pressing my palm to the wood. Through the peephole, I saw him standing there, his head bent against my door. A moment and then two passed, and my heartbeat raced as I thought he was going to knock again. I heard his sigh before he turned and walked down the hall.

He'd said I was dynamite, but he was wrong. It was all him. He'd been the spark that ignited me, and he was the only one whose touch I wanted.

The problem with fires, though, was that they burned fast and furious and usually took out everything in their wake. I feared I would become a casualty.

14

Evan

I stood in my mom's kitchen with Jake, watching as Char and Christina chatted with each other while popping caramel corn for the movie. Already, they'd made a huge batch of kettle corn. The machine in the theater was also filled with buttered popcorn. I prepared myself to gorge on popcorn all night, since Char always made way too much.

Luckily, George had prepared sliders and hot dogs and had already placed them on the sideboard in the theater room.

"Have you seen this?" Jake pulled my attention away from Christina.

I reached for the iPad he held out and read the headline. *Chrisan's Private Dinner: Exclusive photos.*

"A portmanteau? Shit, Jake."

"I like it."

I read the combination of our names again and cringed.

They were shipping us already. I clicked on the article and saw the tasteful pictures Jake had arranged to be taken of us during dinner.

"Not bad." I said as I studied the photographs.

"She's beautiful."

I looked up and met Jake's eyes. He smiled from ear to ear. Ignoring my glare, he held out his hand for the device. He was messing with me, and shit if I hadn't risen to the bait.

"You all set for Thursday?" Jake changed the subject.

I nodded. "Yeah, I'll meet you at the strip at seven."

I glanced at Christina again, who was still laughing at something Char was telling her. I felt the tightening in my chest and knew immediately it was because I didn't want to be away from her this weekend. Walking away from her last night had felt like walking off the field after a loss. I'd have liked nothing more than to spend the night with her, making love to her.

"What can I expect?" I asked Jake.

"They're interested, Evan. This could be big for you. Seth and Jonas MacMillan both have the Midas touch. People love their company, and they love you. It's a perfect partnership."

I nodded. Jake and I had been working on this endorsement deal for six months. If I had to diversify, I only wanted to tie my name to brands that I personally cared about. MacMillan Brothers was a cool company. The two brothers reminded me of my family and our close-knit relationship. Personally, I used several of their lifestyle products, from their workout gear to their casual clothing. I wanted to partner with them. I stood to make a lot as their spokesperson, but it wasn't just about the money. It was about the accomplishment of running my business, which was my brand, profitably. An endorsement deal with MacMillan Brothers was only the beginning for me. I had several business interests I was contemplating, on my terms. The timing had to be right. For now, I could simply enjoy many lucrative years as their lifestyle brand ambassador. Our partnership would require me to travel to San Francisco about once a month for a week, tops, since the contract specified that I have a presence in their hometown, but it wasn't anything that I couldn't uphold.

I wasn't leaving Houston. My family was here. I glanced at Christina again. She was explaining something to Char, who was staring at her in rapt attention. No doubt, the information would work its way into one of Char's books.

My parents walked in then, followed by Max. I saw Christina stiffen and falter midsentence as her eyes connected with Max's.

"Hey, you guys made it." I greeted my mom with a hug and then my dad. I nodded at Max, who lifted an eyebrow sardonically before moving over to the fridge and pulling out a beer. My older brother was such a dick. "How was Hope, Texas?"

"Beautiful," Mom said.

"Unchanged," Dad muttered at the same time.

We all laughed. It was a running joke among them that Mom didn't mind the quiet and peace found in the small Texas town she'd grown up in, while the quiet, slow pace, and old-fashioned feel of the country town gave my dad the jitters. Even in retirement, he preferred a faster pace.

Mom frowned at him before walking over to Char and Christina and the pot of popcorn and brown sugar they were stirring. "Well, we wouldn't miss tonight's feature for anything." She dropped an arm around Char's shoulders, pulling her against her for a hug. "I'm proud of you, darling. Your first film adaptation. We can't wait to see it."

Char kissed Mom on her cheek.

"Hello, Christina. It's good to see you again. How have you been?" My mom hugged Christina briefly as well, and I saw the surprise and the pleasure on her face a second before she hugged Mom back.

"I'm good, thank you."

"You should come for Sunday dinner this weekend."

"Ah, we'll see, Mom." I jumped in before my mom derailed my weekend plans.

Both Mom and Christina looked over at me questioningly.

"Are we watching a movie or what?" Max asked from his position against the refrigerator door.

"We are!" Char declared.

The moment to explain was lost as everyone grabbed a bowl of the caramel corn and trekked out of the kitchen.

I grabbed Christina's hand and held her back. "We can have dinner with Mom next weekend. I'm planning something for us this weekend. I'll tell you more about it later."

Her face lifted and a smile spread across her gorgeous lips. "Okay." She nodded.

I saw the tension go out of her shoulders. I leaned down and kissed her full on the lips. When I lifted my head, she was as red as a beet. She glanced around the kitchen, verifying we were alone.

"Come on. If I've timed this correctly, the only seats left are in the back of the room."

She laughed out loud. "Evan, we are not making out during this movie."

I smirked and lifted an eyebrow.

"I mean it!"

I laughed as I led her out of the kitchen. I realized luck was on my side when we walked into my mom and dad's media room and found that, indeed, the back row of seats was empty. Mom and Dad, Char and Jake had settled in the first row. Max was sitting on the aisle seat on the second row, and the four chairs on the third riser were completely empty. I led Christina to the back two middle loungers. I heard her giggle. Hey, there was no shame in my game.

"You know, when you invited me to dinner and a movie tonight, I had no idea it was an advanced screening of Char's *Russian Roulette*."

"Jake was instrumental in putting together Char's deal with the studio. And he reps Michael McKnight. This sneak peek was happening one way or another."

"This is so awesome." Her eyes were bright with excitement. I leaned down to kiss her and felt like I'd scored a touchdown when her lips parted for me as the lights dimmed and the screen light filled the room.

"You're so beautiful."

"Thank you." She settled into the chair, placing the bowl of popcorn on her lap.

I reached over and grabbed a handful, enjoying when our hands bumped together in the bowl. Out of the corner of my eye, I saw her look down at our hands, then at me before smiling and focusing on the screen again.

The movie adaptation was good. McKnight was in top form. I felt pride for my baby sister. Her novel had been a blockbuster, and she already had devoted fans—like Christina—who read everything she published voraciously. But I dared to bet that my sister's fan base was about to explode with new readers who would rush out to find more of her work after watching this movie.

I linked my hand with Christina's. Hers were soft and

warm. So capable. They reminded me of my mom's hands. Strong, capable, beautiful. I liked that the two of them got along well together. In fact, most everyone in my family loved Christina. Even George treated her with courtesy.

I glanced over at my brother. He was staring at the screen, his head back against his headrest. I wondered if he was even paying attention. I didn't like his indifference toward Christina. Soon, we were going to have a chat about it. Preferably when Dad wasn't around.

I kissed Christina on the top of her head, and she leaned her head against my shoulder, never taking her eyes off the screen. She was loving this. I felt pride that I could give her this moment. I thought of this weekend and what I wanted to do for us. I would make it a weekend to remember. One that would be worthy of her.

All too soon, the credits began scrolling across the screen. We stood up, clapping and cheering for Char.

"Well done, baby girl." Dad pulled Char into a tight hug even as Mom pecked her on her cheek.

"That's going to be a hit, Char. I wouldn't be surprised if you get an option for the second film."

"I pay you to say that, Jake. Christina, you're one of my biggest fans. Did we do the book justice?"

All eyes swung to her, and I felt her stiffen next to me. I wrapped my arm around her shoulder and pulled her closer.

She smiled, nodded. "It was awesome. Michael McKnight nailed Cameron. And the movie followed the book so closely. It was exactly how I pictured it in my mind when I was reading it."

Jake, Mom, and Dad cheered.

"There you have it, Char! Your first honest review from a

fan. I'm proud of you, sis." Max kissed her on the cheek.
"Later, folks." He waved as he walked out of the room.

Dad and Mom followed him out. Jake hugged Char and
promised to be in touch. Soon it was just the three of us in
the room.

"I'm proud of you, Char."

"I am too." Christina hugged her.

"I think I'll watch it again." Char laughed. "By the way,
are you still coming tomorrow night?"

Shit! I'd clean forgotten about Mom's gala tomorrow
night and my one function at the event every year. I nodded,
but I knew she saw the grimace on my face.

"Bring Christina," she said.

I saw Christina's puzzled look. "Mom's fundraising gala
for her medical foundation is tomorrow night. You might
enjoy it. A room filled with a bunch of doctors and surgeons
who are supposed to be the best in their field."

"Say you'll come, Chris. You can keep me company.
Mom's busy working the room and Dad's always by her side.
Max disappears five minutes after he arrives, and well,
Evan's usually on the chopping block. Hey, are you still
doing that this year?"

"Doing what?" Christina laughed, though I saw the
frown crease her forehead. She would prefer if we weren't
talking circles around her.

"Auction for Mom's philanthropy."

"Oh."

"You've got to come, Chris. What time do you get off
work?"

"I'm off tomorrow, actually."

"Perfect. Why don't you come over tomorrow afternoon?
We can get dressed here."

"I..." Christina looked hugely uncomfortable.

"Ease up, Char. Christina might not want to attend."

"No, it's not that." She paused. "Do you want me there?"

"Absolutely! I didn't ask because I honestly forgot about it. But, yeah, I want you there."

"I'm not sure I have anything to wear."

Char laughed and clapped her hands together. "Don't worry about it! I'll have Persia bring some dresses by. What are you—a size eight?" Christina nodded and Char continued. "This is going to be awesome. Evan, have Nigel bring Christina by in the morning. We'll have a spa day, and then you can meet us here for the ride to the gala."

"Did you just plan all that out?" I teased her, though I kept my eyes on Christina. The tension had ebbed out of her body, and I felt her excitement. She was game for it.

Though I'd forgotten that the family's medical foundation's fundraising gala was tomorrow night, I couldn't forget that I was supposed to be one of the bachelor's on the auctioning block. I wasn't looking forward to dinner with another woman. I wondered if Mom would mind too much if Max stepped in for me. I felt dread in my stomach at the thought of asking Max to do me a favor. Two years running now, I'd been the Kennedy up there. Max always seemed to escape Mom's grip when it came to the bachelor auction. Maybe this was the year that changed.

"Is it okay that I'm coming tomorrow night?" Christina asked in the silent car, as I drove her home.

"Are you kidding? It's more than okay. Another date with you, three nights in a row? I'm a lucky man. And my sister's a genius. Remind me to thank her."

Christina laughed. "Okay. Just checking."

"I love spending time with you, Christina. Don't doubt it. And my family loves you."

"Even Max?"

I shrugged my shoulders, then looked over and laughed. She did, too. I reached across the console and held her hand. "You're wonderful. Utterly and completely beautiful. I'll speak to Max."

She tightened her hold on my hand. "No, please don't do that. I don't want to cause a problem between you two."

"Trust me, my talk with Max is going to be about a lot more than the way he treats you. It's been a long time coming. We need to clear the air."

"I'm sorry."

"It's no big deal. He's my idiot older brother. Always has been." I saw her raised eyebrow and her teeth nibbling on her bottom lip. I brushed my thumb over her hand hoping to ease some of her worry. "Don't you ever fall out with Nadia and Fey?"

Her eyebrows drew together as she thought about it. Then she shook her head. "No. Honestly we don't. I mean we don't agree about everything, but we usually go at it until we're hugging in the end."

"Well, you three are remarkably well adjusted then. Max and I hold secret grudges for months on end until one of us gets tired of it or we sense Dad's about to step in, and then we corner the other and force a resolution."

"Sounds very healthy." She laughed.

"I love him. He's an ass, but he's my big brother."

"You're pretty amazing, Evan Kennedy."

I felt the tightening in my chest at the praise in her voice. "So are you, Christina Hart."

When I walked her to her front door and kissed her goodnight, I felt heat and desire explode through my body. But I also felt the overriding emotion of contentment and excitement.

"Have fun with Char tomorrow. I can't wait to see you in the evening."

"Thank you, Evan."

I kissed her again, because I wanted more than her gratitude. More of what, exactly, I didn't know. I didn't dare give it a name.

"Good night, Christina."

"Good night, Evan."

I waited until she closed the door before turning and walking away. I took the stairs down a level and then out into the hallway and through another side door to the parking garage.

We were all falling for Christina. This was supposed to be short-lived. But with every moment, Christina wove herself deeper into the tapestry of my life. This had started as a ruse for the media. But "Chrisan" was very much alive and real. Walking away was going to be difficult.

15

Christina

 he next day, Nigel dropped me off at Char's around one in the afternoon. The media was still hit or miss around my condo, but Nigel had been assigned to me indefinitely it seemed. At least while I remained with Evan.

George opened the front door for me and stepped aside to let me in.

"Miss Char is in the library."

"Hey, Chris!" Char stuck her head out of the library's doorway, a smile on her face.

I embraced her as I walked into the room, which was a mirror image of Evan's. She had a fire going, and she'd been curled up on the couch with her laptop.

"Are you writing?"

She laughed. "Ugh, don't go all fangirl on me. Do you know that's the number one question I get from fans when I'm online or out and about? Everyone wants to know if I'm working on the next novel, or worse, why I'm not at home writing at that very minute."

"What can I say? We love your work. We're addicted to you."

A shadow crossed her face, and her smile faltered slightly.

"I'm sorry. Did I say something wrong?"

Char waved her hand dismissively. "Have you eaten?" she asked, walking past me and out into the foyer, heading for the kitchen.

"I had breakfast."

"I think George made lasagna for lunch."

"Oh, I've had George's lasagna before. It's delicious."

"Thank God for George's cooking!"

She grabbed mittens and pulled the lasagna out of the oven. Then she got plates and cut us both a piece of the delicious-smelling pasta. We sat together at the kitchen table and took a bite of the meaty dish. We both sighed and then burst into laughter.

"So *good*." Char took another bite.

We ate, keeping up easy, companionable conversation. I didn't quiz Char about her writing again, though I wanted to ferret plot secrets out of her about the next book in the series. Instead, I answered her questions about my job as a nurse and some of the things I'd seen during my shifts at the hospital.

Forty minutes passed, and we'd just finished eating, when George came into the kitchen to tell us that Persia had arrived.

Char jumped to her feet. "Thanks, George!"

I stood too, picking up my plate to take it to sink, but George stopped me with his words. "Leave it, Miss Christina. I'll take care of it."

I felt the heat in my cheeks. I wasn't used to people cleaning up after me. Char was already gone from the room. "Oh. Okay. Thank you, George."

"You're welcome." He nodded.

I glanced over my shoulder as I walked out of the kitchen. George was already clearing the table.

I found Char in the foyer, chatting with a young woman who was a little taller and a lot skinnier than me. She had platinum-blonde hair and brilliant blue eyes that zeroed in on me the moment I appeared. She openly stared at me, sizing me up from head to toe. I spotted a rack of clothing against the wall of the foyer.

Char looked over at me. "Christina, this is Persia,—our stylist."

"It's a pleasure to meet you, Christina. The photos don't do you justice. You're gorgeous."

I frowned. I couldn't tell if she was being sincere or only being nice because Char was present. "Thank you," I murmured, turning toward the rack of clothing.

Char was already flipping through the dresses.

"I've got a few pieces here that will be perfect for you, Christina. Char, where should we do this?"

"The guest room, just through here." Char led us down a hallway. She opened a bedroom door and stepped aside so that I could enter and Persia could push the rack of dresses into the room. Only then did she close the door behind her and lean against it.

"We have two hours to find the perfect dress. Stephan comes at three."

I had no idea who Stephan was. As I watched Persia pull a dress off the rack, I doubted I would need two hours. This one was gorgeous, and I wanted to take it home with me.

"Try this on. Through there." Persia pointed toward the bathroom.

"Okay. This is seriously gorgeous."

"This one is just the beginning. You should see what else I've got for you."

I laughed, suddenly feeling years younger. The last time I'd brought a fancy dress had been for Fey's graduation ceremony, and even then, I'd gone to the mall and pulled the first one off the rack that had caught my eye. I didn't usually try on ball gowns, and I certainly didn't do it in a private fitting. To be honest, I might never go back to shopping at the mall again. I wanted to ask Persia what her going rate was but closed the door behind me instead.

I hung the dress up on the hook on the back of the bathroom door. Quickly, I undressed and then put the dress on.

This dress was a strapless, backless, sapphire-blue creation made of satin that hugged my breasts and my torso before flaring slightly at my hips and falling like a waterfall to the floor. I was short and would probably need heels to help keep the dress from dragging on the ground too much. But, against my skin, with my black hair falling loosely past my shoulders, I looked good.

I opened the bathroom door. Two pairs of eyes swung to me. Char clapped her hands together and gave a low wolf whistle.

"Whoa, Christina. You look beautiful. I love it."

"I do, too." I twirled around, giving them a view of the back.

Persia pulled another dress off the rack and handed it to me. "Here, try this one."

I took the dress but shook my head. "I think I'm good."

"You can't choose the first dress you try on. It's the

cardinal rule. You've got to try on at least five, and if the first still trumps, then you go with that. Okay?"

"Yes, ma'am." She was the expert. I walked back into the bathroom. I was loathe to take the dress off. But nevertheless, I placed it back on the hanger and hung it up on the bathroom door hook.

I slipped the red sequined dress over my head and pulled the spaghetti straps over my shoulders. The formal mermaid dress fell to the floor, sparkling under the bathroom lights. The V-neck displayed my ample cleavage. The candy-apple red was a spectacle against my skin. I exhaled as I studied myself in the mirror. It was sexy as hell. But the thought of wearing this dress in front of Evan's mom and dad, at a fundraiser for her medical foundation, left me feeling exposed.

I opened the door and stepped out of the bathroom. Persia's mouth formed a perfect O. Char's eyes went wide.

"Too much?" I asked.

"Oh, you're going home with that dress alright," Char said. "Because Evan's got to see you in it. But I don't think he's going to want anyone else to see you in it."

She and Persia giggled, and I found myself laughing with them. Yeah, the red dress was a bit much for my boyfriend's mom's gala.

Boyfriend? Where had that word come from? Evan wasn't my boyfriend. Why had I just put that label on our relationship?

I accepted the third dress that Persia handed me and walked back into the bathroom. Like the first dress, this one was sapphire, though it was silk and fell straight to my feet. It hugged and showcased every inch of my curves. Though it wasn't overly flashy like the red dress, it too felt like something that was best for just Evan and me out on a date.

I opened the bathroom door and spread my arms wide, turning around slowly so they could see all the angles of the dress.

"You're going home with that one too," Char teased.

"Char! I can't take all these dresses."

"Sure, you can. Don't worry, Evan will thank me. Now, Persia, unless you've got something else up your sleeve, I think Christina's found her dress and it's my turn."

Persia pulled another dress off the rack. "One more." She handed it to me.

Quietly, I walked into the bathroom and changed into the silver dress. The formal, long dress had a bateau neckline and a fitted bodice and skirt. It had ombre silver beading, a low V-back, and a high skirt slit in the back.

It was beautiful. No, past beautiful. It was glorious. No word described the way I felt wearing this dress. It was too easy to say I felt like a princess, or a million bucks, or a diamond. In this dress, I felt like a star shooting across the night sky. Bright, beautiful, unstoppable.

I stepped out of the bathroom and smiled.

Char walked over to me and hugged me. "You're beautiful," she whispered.

"Thank you." I whispered, too.

I hugged Persia as well, and then we were all three laughing. I felt like I imagined Cinderella had felt on her way to the ball. Light, carefree, beautiful, and magical. Sure, Cinderella had only had until midnight, and I was on a deadline, too. But in this moment, none of that mattered. I stared down at the silver dress. I ran my palms over the beading and felt my curves beneath the dress. My body felt beautiful in the dress. For the first time in a long time, I felt beautiful, and it didn't feel like a lie. It felt real. As real as the dress I was wearing tonight.

"Shoes!" Char declared.

Persia snapped her fingers. "I've got the perfect pair."

The strappy, silver sandals with red sole bottoms looked like they'd been made to go with the dress. And they fit perfectly, too. I didn't ask how Persia new my sizes. Frankly I didn't care. She could be a real-life fairy godmother and I wouldn't care. Tonight was mine to enjoy. To hell with the details.

Soon we were saying goodbye to Persia and hello to Stephan, who was going to do our hair and makeup. I felt like a princess getting ready for her ball. I knew all balls ended, but I decided right then and there that I would enjoy every minute of tonight, no matter what it brought.

16

Evan

I watched Christina walk down my parents' staircase and didn't even wonder what she'd been doing upstairs to begin with. She looked magical. Her hair was piled high on top of her head. I met her almond-shaped eyes and held them as she glided down the staircase to stand in front of me. I was aware of Char standing at the top of the stairs watching, the smile on her face. Of course, this was her doing. I would thank her later.

I took the last two steps to Christina. Then I cupped the back of her neck, lowered my lips to hers, and kissed her like we were the only two people in the room. I heard her in drawn breath a moment before she parted her lips and let me in. She tasted of mint and Christina.

"You look beautiful."

"Thank you. You look good, too."

"Thank you, Char!" I called to my sister, not taking my eyes off Christina.

Char laughed as she walked down the stairs. "My pleasure, big brother." Then she walked out the front door, leaving us alone.

I seized the moment. "Christina, before we go. There's something I need to tell you." I saw the question in her eyes and continued. "First, thank you for coming with me tonight. I already know this is going to be my most enjoyable gala ever."

She smiled, and her cheeks flushed slightly. I swallowed, suddenly more nervous than I've ever been, even on game day.

"So, two things: I'm on the auction block tonight—bachelor auction." She nodded. "Sorry, I tried to get around it, but..." I shrugged, remembering how Max had hung up on me today before I could even finish asking him to stand in for me.

She swallowed. "What's the second thing?"

"I have an out-of-town meeting tomorrow. San Francisco." Her face fell. The smile dimmed in her eyes. "It's something that was arranged long before this—us—happened. It's an endorsement deal I've had in the works for months now. The final meeting's tomorrow. I can't change it. But I was hoping that you could fly out and meet me on Friday evening, when you get off work."

I watched the wrinkle between her eyebrows deepen. I wanted to run my thumb over it and smooth it out.

"I don't know if I can afford that."

I laughed and kissed her. "I wasn't clear. I want to take you away for the weekend. I want to surprise you with a getaway. Will you let me?"

She opened her mouth but then hesitated. No words came out. Staring into her eyes, I saw the desire to say yes warring with her fear of the unknown. "Is this part of Jake's plan?"

I felt the buzz of irritation. "No, this has nothing to do with Jake. Or his fake-relationship plot to make us both look good in the media. In fact, if I have my way, no one will know where we are. This weekend is just about you and me, spending time together. I hope it'll be like last weekend, just you and me, maybe a pool."

"Can I give you my answer at the end of the night?"

I watched the emotions running across her face. Saw how she nibbled on her lower lip. "Fair enough."

I wasn't going to give up. If she said no, I would ask her again. I would call her from San Francisco tomorrow, and Friday itself, and I would ask her again. Christina was worth pursuing.

I tucked her hand into the crook of my elbow and escorted her out my parents' home. George and Char were waiting in the front seat of my father's Bentley. I opened the back door for Christina and then slipped in next to her as she slid farther along the seat.

I reached for her hand and held it in mine as George drove away from the house. Soon we were out of McKnight Grove and driving down the oak-lined streets toward the Galleria area and the hotel where Mom's fundraiser was being held this year. We'd be early, but Mom preferred walking into the ballroom and seeing our familiar faces in the room. George would return later to give us a ride home. Mom and Dad usually stayed in a suite at the hotel, since she often assisted the foundation staff with wrap-up.

We would have to make a detour to drop Christina home. There was an unsettling feeling in my gut. I wished she was coming home with me tonight. I glanced at her, but she was peering out her window as the city blurred past.

She looked beautiful tonight. Char's team had done an awesome job. Maybe I could arrange to have them pick up a few pieces for our weekend getaway. I couldn't believe I was thinking so much about this weekend. The night hadn't even ended, and already I was planning the next time I would spend with Christina.

How strange was it that I wanted her company so much? Me, who had spent the past four years avoiding any kind of intimacy with a woman, was craving this woman's presence. It was all Christina. I had no idea what about her had caught my eye so completely. It wasn't her physical beauty. She was beautiful, but I'd seen beautiful women before. That hadn't been what had reached across that restaurant's floor and held me spellbound as she walked to her seat. There was an unfamiliar, magnetic force to Christina that totally captivated me. I sensed it whenever I was close to her. And when I was away from her, I just wanted to be with her.

Was I lonely? Was that what this was? I'd spent four years avoiding women altogether. I don't think my family or my friends knew the extent to which I had withdrawn after the incident with Isabelle. Going on a date with a woman, seducing her and being seduced by her, had held little appeal. Until Christina, that is.

I lifted her hand to my lips. She turned her head to face me, and I saw the flare of desire in her eyes. Christina was as attracted to me as I was to her. I held her gaze. I kissed the inside of her wrist. Then I leaned down and kissed that sweet spot just below her ear, before her collarbone. I felt the ripple of desire flow down her body and received its echo in mine.

Where was this heading? Hell, if I knew. We were attracted to each other. We also liked each other. It was more than just physical desire. I'd spent a weekend with her, taken her over to my parents—twice now—and I couldn't stand the thought of another man anywhere near her.

What was I doing? I didn't have a clue. I could be setting myself up for heartbreak. What if things went sideways with Christina? Would she drag me through the media? If someone came to her with a good offer, would she turn on me for the cash? People did hurtful things when they were hurting. Wasn't that why I had avoided relationships these past four years? The last thing I wanted was to hurt Christina. But what if I invariably did end up hurting her?

How long could this relationship run for? Three months? Just enough for the media attention to die down, for another couple to claim the spotlight. What happened when that external force demanding that Christina and I spend time together wasn't a factor anymore? Would she still want to spend time with me?

Damn! My thoughts were depressing the hell out of me. I didn't want to think that far out. Hell, I barely knew what I was doing *now*. Best to just get through tonight, with its bachelor auction and all the intelligent, medical personnel and the boring and sometimes gory stories they would tell tonight. Best to focus on the beautiful woman by my side and enjoy yet another lovely memory with her.

17

Christina

$\mathcal{T}$he ballroom at the hotel where the gala was being held had been decorated in silver and gold. Balloons, steamers, and flowers were everywhere. The room looked elegant and formal. Couples were as well-dressed as Evan and me, and it felt nice standing next to him. A few people had approached us to say hello and snap a picture with Evan. I kept forgetting he was a very popular football player. Evan didn't act like a celebrity.

The orchestra was playing all the modern songs and it was otherworldly watching couples waltz in formal wear to some of the latest pop melodies. Evan and I stood next to each other, our bodies brushing against each other's, watching the couples dance across the floor.

"My mom has a thing for love songs."

"I love it."

The orchestra started a beautifully familiar melody. It took a minute, but I recognized the popular song at the same time that Evan leaned down and whispered in my ear.

"This is how we fall in love."

I felt the warmth flush my cheeks. "This is how *you* fall in love," I corrected him. Then laughed because it was obvious he knew the name of the Jeremy Zucker and Chelsea Cutler song.

"May I have this dance?"

"I don't know how." I shook my head. "And everyone's watching."

"Do you trust me?"

I stared at him. He stood tall and proud in his black tuxedo. He was huge, and he should look clumsy in the outfit, but it fit him so well and he wore it so well that he looked beautiful, like some powerful demigod. He looked as beautiful as I felt in my silver dress. There was a fire shining in his eyes that made them bright and sent a tingle racing up and down my spine.

Did I trust him?

I looked down at his outstretched hand. I felt my stomach dip as realization took hold. I trusted him more than I had ever trusted another man. I placed my hand in his and lifted my head in time to see the slow, sexy smile that crossed his lips before he pulled me closer to him.

He placed his hand on my lower back and wrapped my hand around his neck. He moved forward and I moved back. He pulled me to the right and I followed, then he stepped back and I came forward. He was puppet master, and I was his puppet on a string. It was easy to follow him. And I loved every carefree moment of it.

"Everyone's staring," I murmured to Evan.

They were. Most couples had cleared off the floor and were standing on the edge, still in each other's arms, watching us. I caught sight of Brandy's smile as we whirled by her.

"They should stare. You're beautiful."

I laughed and fully gave myself over to Evan and his rhythm.

All too soon the music ended. Applause broke out. I buried myself in Evan's hug and let him lead me off the dance floor. Conversation erupted, filling the silence left by the musicians who were now packing up their instruments and moving off the raised dais.

"Looks like it's time for me to pay the piper." Evan was frowning as he spoke, and I saw him looking around the room. He looked uncomfortable for the first time that night.

"The auction?" I asked.

He nodded. "Why don't you wait with Mom and Dad while I get through this? I'll make it back to you as soon as I can," he said as we walked toward his parents.

I ignored the hardening in my stomach. For the first time since meeting Evan, I wished I was rich. I envied every single one of the women in the room tonight who would bid on him.

"Oh, Evan, sweetheart, thank you for swapping with Max. I forgot how complicated the auction would be for you this year given your relationship." Brandy smiled at me.

I looked at Evan, but he looked just as confused as I felt.

"I tried, but he hung up on me actually."

A thin line marred Brandy's forehead. "Really? He called Annabelle this afternoon to inform her that he was taking your place at the auction."

Evan shook his head. "But he isn't even here."

"Yes, he arrived about five minutes ago. Look." Brandy gestured across the room. "There he is with Alyssa Montgomery."

I followed Brandy's arm and saw Max standing in the corner of the ballroom next to a tall, stunningly beautiful redhead.

"Alyssa?" Evan's eyebrows shot up.

Mom sighed. "I suspect it's only because he plans to have her bid on him during the auction."

Someone on Brandy's staff interrupted to ask her a question.

"Montgomery as in Montgomery Hotels?" I whispered to Evan.

He nodded. "Also Max's ex."

"Oh."

I took a sip of my champagne as I studied Max and his ex-girlfriend without being too obvious about it. They looked beautiful together: Max—tall, dark, and handsome —and Alyssa—fair and redheaded. They conversed easily, facing each other as if they were the only two in the room. Their interactions spoke of easy friendship. Max was always so somber, so standoffish, it was difficult to imagine that he had friends or that he would even be friends with an ex-girlfriend. But there, across the room, was the proof, laughing at something Max had just said.

"Where's Char?" I asked suddenly, realizing I hadn't seen her for quite some time.

"Gone home. Headache." Paul spoke softly.

I caught the glance he exchanged with Evan, and the answering frown on Evan's face. Was something wrong with Char? I bit my tongue to hold back the questions and made a mental note to ask Evan about it later.

Ten minutes later, when the auction had begun and it was Max's turn, he stepped onto the dais. The spotlight shone brightly on him. I had to admit, he looked rather dashing in his black tuxedo. His hair was cut shorter than the last time I'd seen him, and it was brushed neatly in place. He stood with his hands loosely at his sides, perfectly composed. If the ladies were disappointed by the brothers' switch, I couldn't tell by the murmurs of appreciation filling the room.

"Every year, we're given the opportunity for a romantic date with Evan Kennedy, handsome son of our foundation's president, Brandy Kennedy, and a star in his own right. I don't have to tell you Evan plays tight end offensive for our Houston Texans," the host began. "This year, however, we're breaking with tradition. As we can all see, Evan is off the market. His handsome older brother, Max Kennedy, has graciously offered to step in for Evan, and I am sure that any one of you ladies tonight would be lucky to win a dinner date with Max. Let's start the bidding, shall we?"

"Five thousand." Alyssa lifted her hand and waved.

Most everyone in the room laughed. Max scowled at her.

"Surely, we can do better than that, can't we?" the host joked.

More laughter filled the room, but the ladies took it to heart, and the bidding—and the amount being bidden —increased.

I laughed out loud and shook my head in disbelief when the bidding reached one hundred thousand dollars. Honestly, I'd suffered through a dinner with Max; I wasn't sure he was worth that much. Who were these people who would think nothing of dropping a house down payment for a date with a man?

I caught the glare Max directed at Alyssa and saw her answering shake of the head and the smile on her lips. Max shot out his cuffs and tugged at his collar. Alyssa seemed to take pity on him because she lifted her hand and spoke again.

"Five hundred thousand. And I doubt you'll get a better offer."

"I think she's right," Evan called out.

Laughter and applause sounded in the room. Max didn't wait. He jumped off the dais and then was surrounded by people, shaking his hand and clapping him on the back. He walked straight to Alyssa. She handed him the champagne glass she'd been holding. He drained it and, placing an arm on her lower back, led her over to us.

"Max, that's too much." Brandy hugged him and kissed his cheek. She reached over and kissed Alyssa, too.

"I agree. That wasn't my doing."

"Alyssa. Thank you."

Alyssa smiled and waved her hand dismissively. "You're welcome, Brandy. It's all for a good cause."

Her eyes rested on mine, and I saw the sudden sparkle. "It's nice to meet you."

I frowned as I shook her outstretched hand. Then it dawned on me that she was referring to the media hoopla regarding my relationship with Evan, and her finally having an opportunity to put a person to the news articles.

"Nice to meet you, too." I felt some of my tension ease as Evan wrapped his arm around my waist and pulled me closer to him.

"Mom, we're not staying," Max interrupted. He kissed his mom again on the cheek and then hugged his father. He nodded at Evan, but he barely looked at me as he wrapped his arm around Alyssa's waist and they walked away together.

"We should think about heading out, too," Evan said as Brandy and Paul walked away to chat with another couple.

I nodded. Tonight had been surreal. A true fairy-tale ball. I was loathe to see it end. I knew I would never forget it.

"Do you have an answer for me?"

I held Evan's gaze and took in the way he looked tonight, the tiny hint of a smile curving his mouth upward. I wanted to kiss the corner of his lips. I wanted to run my fingers over his black eyebrows and ease the frown forming between them. I wanted to touch him. And who said I couldn't? Weren't we a couple?

I laid my hand on his tuxedo-covered chest and smoothed my palm over to the top of his shoulder. He took a sharp breath, and something answered in my core. He stepped toward me, and I took a step toward him too, until we were just barely touching.

The orchestra had started playing again. Waiters were moving through the crowd with trays of champagne and platters of tiny bites. None of them mattered or distracted me from my focus on Evan in this moment.

"Yes."

He tilted his head to the side. His palm came to rest on my cheek. I couldn't help turning my face into his large hand. Evan's touch was magical. I loved how it called to something deep inside of me.

"Yes, you have an answer?" He lowered his face to mine.

"Yes is my answer."

He kissed me. The orchestra's music reached a crescendo at that moment, the melody they were playing climaxing in perfect timing to Evan's kiss.

A few moments later, Evan and I said goodbye to Brandy and Paul. George was waiting for us at the curb when we walked out of the hotel's front doors. He held the back door open for us.

"Did Char get home okay?" Evan asked George as I slid across the back seat.

"Yes, Mr. Evan. She was working in her office when I left."

Evan sat next to me. He took my hand and rested it on his thigh.

"Evan, is something wrong with Char?"

Deep lines formed between his brows. "No, I'm sure she's fine."

"I had a wonderful time tonight."

"I did, too. And wait until you see what I have planned for you this weekend."

"I can't wait." I smiled at him.

"I'm out of town tomorrow morning, remember?"

I nodded. Evan lifted my hand to his lips and kissed it, sending warmth flooding through me.

"Do you get off at four on Friday?"

He was kissing the inside of my wrist now. I nodded again. I'd lost my voice, and my breath caught in my throat. Desire pooled at my core.

"Nigel will pick you up. He'll have the details."

"Shouldn't I have the details?" I sounded breathless even to my ears.

Evan shook his head. He leaned down and brushed his lips on the sweet spot below my ear, just above my collarbone, that had totally become his spot. "Not when it's your surprise."

I pulled back, frowning up at him, but he only brushed his thumb between my eyebrows, smoothing out my frown. I shivered at his caress.

"Trust me?"

I nodded. "Yes."

I trusted him.

He was worth trusting.

As he walked me to my door, I searched within myself

and realized the truth. I was ready for the next step I knew was coming in our relationship.

Evan cupped my face and pressed his lips against mine. My thoughts dissolved. I wrapped my arms around his neck, pulling him closer as I lost myself in the feel of his lips against mine. My knees felt weak, and I was thankful when Evan's hands slid down my side to wrap about my waist, holding me tightly against his body. I felt his arousal against my stomach and waited for the spike of anxiety to come, but there was only the thrill of desire.

"I want you," he whispered against my lips.

"I want you, too."

"Not like this though. Not with George waiting for me downstairs. When we make love for the first time, I'm not going to be in a hurry."

"Okay."

He placed a chaste kiss on my lips. "This weekend."

"Yes." It felt like a promise.

We were taking a big step, moving our relationship in a new direction. We were both ready.

18

Christina

I woke up the next morning to the sound of hushed murmuring in the living room. I rolled over and covered my eyes with my palms. Icy-cold wetness flowed through my stomach and sent a tingle racing up my spine. I sat up, the sense of foreboding sending adrenaline coursing through my veins.

I looked around my bedroom, but all seemed in order. I listened to the voices. It was only Nadia and Fey. I pushed my covers aside and walked over to my bedroom door. Opening the door, I stepped into the hallway. My sisters went silent.

"What is it?" I walked over to the couch and sat, tucking my feet beneath me.

Nadia and Fey exchanged a glance. Then Nadia walked over to me and sat on the coffee table. She pulled out her cell phone and tapped a couple times on the screen. It reminded me of last weekend, and I cringed remembering how everything had changed.

She held out the phone to me. My hands were shaking as I took it. I held her eyes for a second before looking down at the screen in my hand.

Christina Hart: From Orphan to Billionaire's Girlfriend. Exclusive details!

I clicked on the headline and quickly read through the article. I felt heat explode in my ears and flow down my face, down my neck, over my chest. There, printed in plain English for everyone to read, was my life's history. The article spared no detail—from my dad walking out on my mom and me when I was five years old, to my mom dying of cancer when I was eight. Details about my stay at the different group homes were mentioned. I breathed a sigh of relief when I noticed that Fey and Nadia hadn't been mentioned in the article. But there was a quote from some "best friend" who had gone to nursing school with me and with whom I had hung out at clubs on some nights, hooking up with random guys. Lies interspersed with facts. The article all but suggested that I'd been trolling clubs looking for a rich boyfriend to hook up with. Lucky for me, naive Evan had come along, and the rest was a media sensation.

I waited for anger and outrage to come. Instead, heavy, crushing embarrassment settled on my shoulders, weighing me down. I felt naked, completely exposed. I held out Nadia's phone. She took it from me and entwined her fingers with mine.

Fey sat next to me and placed a hand on my knee. "Are you okay?"

I shook my head. I wasn't. Those people had written about my life as if they had a right to. That article dissected me as if I weren't a human with actual feelings. Even going so far as to mention the number of group homes I'd stayed in as a minor and, in some cases, even my length of stay. It was embarrassing enough that my private life had just been blasted across the internet for all to read.

"Sweetie, no one who matters will believe this." Nadia squeezed my fingers. I met her eyes and saw anger and fierce protectiveness shining in them.

"Nadia's right. Those who love you wouldn't give a shit about this," Fey seconded.

I wanted to believe them. There was a part of me that wanted to say, "Fuck 'em." She wanted to stand up, lift her head high, and walk into my bedroom, slamming the door behind her. But the part of me that was winning was this one, who was sitting on the couch, feeling smaller than small.

Had Evan read this? Had Jake? Char? Max? There were details in here about my life that I hadn't even shared with Evan. Or the people I worked with. Would they see me as a gold digger? As someone going after Evan for his money? Would Evan think that about me?

People always thought the worst about each other. I'd told Evan I didn't date. Would he think it was because I was holding out for some rich guy? Someone like him? Would Evan see the time we'd spent together as me trying to make a move on him because of his money?

I did stand then. "I have work."

Though I felt sick to my stomach, I walked to my bedroom and shut the door. On autopilot, I went into my bathroom, took a shower, and got dressed for work. Nigel would be here any minute now to pick me up.

The thought of facing my coworkers and the people at the hospital had my stomach turning over. But I wasn't a coward, and there was no place to hide. This was my life. I had a job. I had goals. I was supposed to be building my future. Hiding out at home, waiting for this latest assault to blow over wasn't an option. I didn't hide from my life. I'd never stay in bed with the covers pulled over my head. This too was going to past. And I would be out achieving my goals while it did.

Four hours later, the smile on my face felt like it had been painted on. I stood at the front check-in desk with my head down, transcribing records into the computer. Becky, another nurse who was not as friendly as Amanda or Kayla, sat next to me, minding her own business. The guard, now a permanent fixture at the front desk, did a great job of making sure everyone who approached the desk had a legitimate reason for doing so.

I wasn't being harassed, but I wasn't being ignored either. My skin crawled every time I thought of the details of this morning's article, which spelled out the highlights of my life for anyone to consume.

Was this what Evan had felt like four years ago when he'd been accused of hurting his ex-girlfriend? Had he faced people's unwarranted and unwanted judgments? I couldn't blame him for being secretive about his life following that experience.

"Christina?"

I looked up and saw Brandy standing in front of my desk with the chief of staff by her side.

"Hi!" I exclaimed, moving around the desk. I stopped short, unsure of how I should greet her.

She made the move first, hugging me tightly before pulling away.

"How nice to run into you. I wasn't sure if you were on duty today."

"Ah yes, of course you two would know each other." The

chief of staff stuffed his hands in his pockets, a tight smile on his face.

"Of course, Bill." Brandy laughed. Then she turned back to me and asked, "Do you have time to grab a cup of coffee with me?"

I hesitated, glancing at my coworker first, who was avidly listening to our interaction, and then at the chief, who stood next to Brandy, eyeing me speculatively.

"I'm sure Christina can spare a few minutes," the chief said. His smile still looked tight to me, but it softened as he turned to face Brandy.

"Thank you again for the donation, Brandy. We're grateful beyond words for you and Paul."

"Thank you, Bill. Always a pleasure to see you. Please give my regards to Dianne."

The chief nodded at me before turning and walking away. I met Brandy's smile and wondered what the chances were that she hadn't seen the awful article.

"Is the cafeteria coffee okay? Or did you want to do the coffee cart in the courtyard?" I asked.

"The courtyard's fine. I think it'll be much quieter, too."

The courtyard was all but deserted when we stepped through the open archway. I could hear the falling water in the marble fountain that occupied the center of the outdoor space. At eleven o'clock in the morning, it seemed that everyone else had opted for the cafeteria, and there was no one at the coffee cart. We both got a latte and found an empty bench beneath one of the large trees lining the courtyard space.

"How are you doing?" We'd been sitting quietly on the bench for a minute when Brandy spoke.

The shame that hadn't gone very far all morning, reared itself to the forefront again. Tears filled my eyes. I lifted my coffee cup to my lips and swallowed the milky brew. "If I'm being honest, I've been better."

"Jake tries his best, but it's hard to control the press and how invasive they can be."

"You read the article."

She nodded.

"It's so personal. The things they wrote about me. My childhood, being in foster care—that's all supposed to be private. It isn't something I talk about."

"Fame is hard on a relationship. The press will dig and dig until they find anything they think will feed the public frenzy."

"It's overwhelming. Sometimes it feels like I can't breathe. I don't know how Evan does it. How do you?"

Brandy smiled. "We've had a little more practice than you. Evan went through the fire four years ago. I'm assuming you know?"

I nodded, and she continued. "I thought so. Christina, everything I've seen indicates that you and Evan are friends first and foremost. That friendship will make all the difference. It'll help you navigate everything that comes with a relationship in the spotlight."

I looked down at my coffee cup. I wasn't so sure. Yes, Evan and I were friends. But we were both pushing for more. In fact, we were supposed to be going away for the weekend, and I was pretty sure we were going to take our relationship to the next level.

"Evan is a great guy. He's kind and funny, down to earth. Nothing at all what I imagined a rich football player would be like. He cares. What happens if—no, when—the media decides he could do better than an orphaned gold digger?"

"You and Evan can't live in a bubble. Your relationship exists in the real world, but it is *your* relationship. Nothing the media prints can separate you unless you two stop communicating with each other."

Brandy must have seen my doubt because she continued. "You know I grew up in Hope, Texas, about four hours from Houston, right?" I nodded. "My mom died when I was five. My father raised me alone after Mom died. He was a mechanic. He had his hands full taking care of me and keeping our shop in the black. Most of my time outside of school was spent in the garage with him. I grew up eating a lot of takeout, mostly tacos. Those were my dad's favorite. I didn't mind because he was my favorite. We loved each other. I was so scared when I left to go to college. I'd gotten a full scholarship and Dad insisted that I go. He always wanted more for me than Hope, Texas.

"Christina, it isn't where you come from or how you start, it's what you do with your life—with all the opportunities and curve balls that life throws you. I met Paul at college my first semester. I saw him walk into my undergrad biology class and I swear the ground moved beneath me when our eyes connected. I had no idea who his family was or the toes we would step on when we started dating and then eloped three months later.

"Let's just say I wasn't what anyone, including the media, envisioned for Paul Kennedy. He was being groomed to take over Kennedy Enterprises, and I was a nobody from a small town. He should have married a woman who knew how to throw important dinners for her husband, how to keep a home, and all the right philanthropies to partner with. Instead, he ended up with a wife who couldn't scramble eggs without burning them."

"I've tasted your cooking, Brandy. You're a wonderful cook."

"Turkey, cranberry sauce, green bean casserole." Brandy

suddenly erupted into a fit of laughter. "Didn't you find my menu odd for a Friday night family dinner?"

I frowned, and she laughed. "Our second Thanksgiving together, Paul and I went home to my dad's, and I was determined that we would not eat tacos. I found a cookbook and followed the recipes to the letter. It was the first time I'd cooked anything. And, to this day, those are the only dishes I enjoy cooking. We have George now, thank God! But my family knows that whenever I cook, it's Thanksgiving dishes they're getting."

I laughed. I felt the block of icy shame that had encased my heart since this morning's article begin to melt.

"I can't cook either," I admitted lightly, feeling anything but judged. "I never had the chance to learn how, and honestly, I'm not sure I'd be any good at it. And I can't drive either."

"Then it's a good thing you have Nigel." We laughed together.

Then the reality of the situation hit me. "Evan deserves more," I whispered.

"Evan deserves love. And you do too, Christina. I can imagine the article didn't come close to the truth of what it was like to lose your mom *and* your dad and bounce from home to home. I do know about some of the fears and feelings that come with growing up with the loss of a parent. Don't let fear keep you from a relationship with Evan. You two owe it to yourselves to see what's there."

"We're supposed to spend this weekend together. I'm not sure if it's a good idea. I don't know that I can live this public life he leads."

"I know you're not seeing my son because of what he does for a living or how much money he has in his account. He can't control the media and what they print. He and Jake try, they do, really hard. But, when it comes to the media, you must have thick skin. I may be biased, but Evan is worth it, Christina. Don't give up on him because of something he can't control."

"I know he's worth it." Brandy wasn't telling me anything I hadn't thought of before. I guess the question was whether I was good enough for Evan, and for his life.

"And, Christina, you are worth it, too. He's lucky to have you because you care about him for the man he is. You're not moved by the size of his bank account or the trappings of wealth that come with dating him. You are rare. And he's lucky to have found a woman like you. Give your relationship the chance it deserves."

I thought about our conversation for the remainder of the day. I met Nigel in the garage at the end of my shift and sat silently in the back of the black Tahoe as he drove me home.

"I'll see you at six tomorrow morning. But call me if you need me before then."

"Thank you, Nigel. I appreciate it."

I closed the door to my apartment behind me and turned the lock. The space was quiet. Fey and Nadia were not home yet. I went straight to my bathroom. I pulled off my scrubs and placed them in the hamper. The water was hot and soothing on my head. I let it flow over me until the room was full of steam and the tensions of the day were swirling down the drain.

Later, when I crawled into bed, I reached for my phone and unlocked the screen. Social media had been my least favorite thing before I'd started dating Evan. Now, I had zero interest in checking my pages. I didn't want to read the comments or see the articles my "friends" had tagged me in. I stayed away from the web browsers as well, certain that some story about me would occupy the home pages. I was about to put the phone back on my nightstand when a notification came through.

I clicked on the message.

Evan: I'm sorry about the article. How are you doing?

Me: I'm okay. How was your meeting?

Evan: Good. I can't wait to see you tomorrow and tell you all about it.

I hesitated. I'd told his mom I would give us a chance. But it still felt a little like I was delaying the inevitable. My phone beeped again, and this time Evan had sent me a link.

I clicked on it and watched as a news video clip of Evan and Jake walking through a group of reporters filled the screen. They were walking toward a building, a black SUV at their backs. Reporters were all around with cameras and microphones, obstructing the walkway.

A female reporter shoved a microphone in Evan's face. "Evan, what do you make of the rumors about Christina's past? That she's with you for your money?"

Evan stopped walking. He looked at the reporter, then shifted his gaze to the camera.

"Christina has overcome the odds stacked against her to succeed in life. She's a remarkable woman. She doesn't need a handout from me. I'm lucky to have her in my life."

Tears filled my eyes at the sight of Evan defending me. He'd read the worst about me, and he'd taken my side. Publicly. He'd taken a stand for me and our relationship. Now, the question remained—what was I going to do?

I'd always avoided relationships with men. Dating and getting close to anyone had never been a desire of mine. In fact, I'd pushed plenty of people away, keeping friends and coworkers at a distance. Evan had been a first, and he'd brought so many wonderful people into my life: Char,

Brandy, Nigel. They were friends. People I enjoyed but would never have known had I not opened up to Evan.

I thought everyone left eventually, but perhaps it was only because I was pushing everyone away. Was I setting myself up to end up alone, much like I thought I would? Was I creating a self-fulfilling prophecy?

I didn't want to end up alone. I wanted love and companionship and friendship. I wanted more of what I'd found with Evan. I wanted it to be real, and I wanted it to last.

Me: I can't wait to see you too.

It was the truth. I wanted this weekend getaway with Evan. I couldn't wait to see him and be with him again. Was I opening myself up to be hurt? Sure. It was a strong possibility. But it was a risk I was willing to take. Some things in life were worth the risk. Evan was one of them.

19

Christina

The trip to Napa Valley on Friday evening was quiet and uneventful, a definite perk of traveling on a private jet. The Cessna Citation X—which is what Nigel called the plane—was sleek, beautiful, and quick. We were the only two passengers in the cabin, which could seat six. Nigel settled me in one of the seats in the middle of the plane and then claimed a seat at the back. I was glad for the solitude. I spent most of the three hours and twenty minutes of the flight napping, only waking up when Nigel sat in the seat across the aisle from me.

"We're descending now."

I looked out the window, my breath catching at the sight of the green pastures, busy freeway, and the patches of water. Soon the plane was touching down and slowing down as it ate up the runway in front of it.

The plane taxied to a stop in front of a hanger. There, standing in front of a large black SUV, were Evan and Jake.

My breath caught at the sight of Evan. He stood tall by the hood of the vehicle, dressed in a white shirt and khaki trousers. God, he was so hot.

"Hi." I approached him.

"Glad you came."

Nigel brought my bags over and placed them in the trunk of the car. Jake murmured something to Evan before walking past me with a wave and boarding the plane.

"Have fun, kids!" Nigel tipped an imaginary hat as he too turned away and boarded the plane.

"He's not staying?"

"Hardly." Evan reached for my hand and pulled me closer to him. His lips descended on mine, hesitantly at first, before demanding a response from me. I forgot where we were. I didn't care who was watching. Evan's mouth, his lips pressing against mine, was all that mattered.

Evan lifted his head, cupped my cheeks with his hands. "It's good to see you."

I nodded. My tongue felt like a foreign object in my mouth. I let him guide me to the SUV. He held the front door open for me, and I climbed into the passenger seat.

I alternated between watching the scenery outside our car window and watching Evan as he drove away from the airport. He asked me about work, and I filled him in half-heartedly. I'd spent most of yesterday and today cringing through the day, so I didn't really want to talk about it.

Before too long, we were driving through two open metal gates and up a gravel road lined with fields of green. A sprawling, three-story mansion stood at the end of the driveway. I counted thirteen large windows with white wooden shutters against the red brick of the house.

"It's beautiful!"

"Welcome to McKenzie Estate."

I saw Evan's pride in the vineyard in the easy smile curving his lips and the relaxed way he glided the car to a stop at the bottom of wide, climbing stone stairs. Two men stood at the top of the stairs, one wore comfortable jeans and a button-down shirt, and the other wore a business suit.

Both men walked down the stairs toward us as we stepped out of the SUV. I walked around the front of the car to stand next to Evan.

"Evan, good to see you, man!"

The man in jeans shook Evan's hand and embraced him briefly, clasping his back with his other hand.

"Justin! Thanks for arranging this on such short notice."

"Anytime. You must be Christina. It's a pleasure to meet you."

I shook his hand, wondering if he too had read the articles about Evan and me.

He smiled warmly at me though. There was no judgment or speculation in his expression. "Bags in the trunk?"

"Yes."

Evan handed him the keys and reached for my hand. Justin tossed the keys to the man in the suit, who walked to the trunk of the SUV and began to unpack our bags.

"I put you guys in the corner rooms on the top floor. We're not fully booked but that should give you even more privacy."

I felt heat climbing up my cheeks, but Evan only thanked Justin again and wrapped his arm around my shoulders, leading me inside.

The house was beautiful—wooden panels on the walls, crown moldings on the high ceilings, crystal chandeliers that threw light everywhere and shone like a thousand diamonds in the huge space. Evan and I followed Justin up the wide stairs to the top floor. Evan's ease told me he was familiar with the place.

Justin stopped in front of a door at the end of the hallway and turned the knob, then held the door open for Evan and me to walk through. The room first opened into the living room space, complete with a sofa, two chairs, and a coffee table in the middle. There was a bedroom on either side of the living room.

I felt a bit of relief upon realizing that we had separate bedrooms. Then I found myself wondering why we had separate bedrooms. I walked away to explore the bedroom on my right just as a couple bellhops brought our bags in.

The bedroom was a large suite with floor-to-ceiling windows. A padded bench with intricately carved legs sat at the foot of a king-sized poster bed. A door led to the private bathroom. The claw-foot tub sitting in the middle of the room was beautiful, as was the spacious tiled shower with two showerheads. I walked out of the bedroom in time to hear Evan thanking Justin as they walked toward the door. The bellhops were already gone.

"This is great, man. Thank you."

"My pleasure, Evan. We're holding a table on the balcony for you. And everything's been arranged for tomorrow."

Evan shook hands with Justin.

"Let me know if you need anything else," he said as he exited.

Now it was just the two of us.

Evan spread his arms wide, palms up. "What do you think?"

"This place is amazing. I expected a house on a hill, but I didn't expect this."

Evan laughed. "My father doesn't do anything in half

measures. The first floor has a huge restaurant with a fully loaded kitchen that serves the guests who stay here or come through for tours of the winery. The top two floors are rooms that can be rented."

I walked over to him and slipped my hands into his open palms. "So, two bedrooms, huh?"

He smiled and wrapped my arms around his waist. His hands trailed up my arms before cupping my face. He leaned down and kissed me. His lips devoured mine as his hands trailed down to my back, pressing me fully against him.

Heat blazed through my body, igniting a path that led straight to my core. The latest media attack, the uncertainty of what might come, the knowledge that I was losing my heart to Evan, all of it faded to black. There was only the two of us and the singular emotion coursing between us.

Evan tore his lips from mine, trailing kisses along my jaw, my neck, and back up to my mouth again. He pulled free with a deep indrawn breath and pressed his forehead against mine.

"Come on," he said suddenly, taking my hand and leading me toward the door. "I made dinner reservations for us downstairs."

Our dinner was served at a quiet table for two on a secluded part of the balcony overlooking a sprawling garden, which gave way to the vineyard. The outdoors was well lit, and I could see the perfect landscape that went on and on for as far as the eye could see.

"How large is the estate?"

"Eighty-eight acres altogether."

"That's huge."

"It holds its own for an underdog."

I didn't know much about wines—just like I didn't know

much about scotch—but I knew what tasted good, and the wine we'd enjoyed at Bartholomew's on the Bayou had been delicious.

"Justin oversees all of the estate operations. He manages the winemaker and the vineyard manager to make sure production stays on track and we're turning a profit."

"Sounds like he's got his hands full."

"He does. McKenzie Estate wouldn't be successful without him. He takes the pressure off our family."

"You know a lot about the estate yourself."

"It's one of my favorite businesses."

Dinner was delicious. Evan told me more about his business meeting with the MacMillan Brothers and the deal he'd finalized with them. He was now officially their spokesperson.

"So, am I going to see your face in magazines and on billboards now?"

He shrugged his sexy shrug and smiled. "Maybe a few." He sipped his wine, placed the glass down, and toyed with the stem. "Mostly, it's a way for me to make my own mark when it comes to business. Do some things outside of K.E. and football."

"You're pretty awesome, Evan. Not at all what I thought you'd be."

He reached across the table and took my hand in his. "You're pretty amazing too, Christina Hart. You're everything I imagined you'd be. So much more."

I breathed in deeply and tightened my hand around his. His words caused a flutter of excitement in my stomach. I had to ask because I needed to know where we stood.

"If you've already closed on your deal, where does that leave our fake romance?"

He lifted my hand to his lips and kissed it. Turning my

hand over, he kissed the inside of my wrist in just that spot that always left me breathless. His eyes never left mine. "I wasn't pursuing a fake romance when I brought you here."

"No?" I breathed.

"No. I was hoping for something real with you."

We had crossed the line. Stepped into new territory. The pretending was over. We liked each other, enough to want to know what was possible. No matter what happened next, Evan had already left his mark on me. He wasn't anything I'd planned, but he was so much better than any plan I could have conceived.

He held my hand as we walked back to our suite. He unlocked the door, and I walked in ahead of him. I should have felt nervous, but there was only an overwhelming feeling of rightness. No ounce of anxiety, caution, or worry about what-ifs. Just the certainty that I cared deeply for Evan.

I came to standstill in the middle of the living room and asked him the question I'd asked him earlier tonight.

"Two bedrooms?"

He smiled as he walked over to me. He brushed a lock of hair behind my ear, cupped my cheek in his palm.

"Only if you need it."

My heart skipped a beat before settling into a sure rhythm. He was leaving the next move up to me. Despite his obvious desire for me, he wasn't going to rush me. I felt an emotion unfurl in my heart, leaving me warm and tingling inside. It burst through me like sunlight coming through a shroud of clouds. It was love. A love that was strong and deep. It demanded that I lift my hands to Evan's cheeks, trace my fingers across his strong jaw. It demanded that I let him know just how I felt about him.

"I don't need it."

A slow smile spread across his lips. I pulled his face down toward me and kissed him, deeply, soundly. I told him, with my lips, everything that my heart had already decided moments ago. I felt my feet leave the floor. It took me a moment to realize that Evan had picked me up and was carrying me toward his bedroom. It felt wonderful being in his arms, surrounded by him. Like safety and heat colliding. It felt like coming home.

I groaned at the thought. He set my feet on the carpet. I pulled his shirt out of his khakis, my fingers working the buttons. Slowly, I got them undone, and then my palms were pressed flat against his muscular chest. I moved closer to him, wanting more of his warmth. He was heaven to touch. Better than anything I had imagined.

Long moments passed in a flash as we stripped each other of our clothing. His hands explored and caressed each curve as I held onto his firm flesh, feeling the pressure climbing and climbing, until we were panting, fighting to catch a breath.

We fell on the bed together, dressed only in our underwear. Evan paused, his hands on either side of me, holding his weight off me. I stroked the muscles in his strong arms, felt the answering ripple through his body.

His gaze roamed over me from head to toe before meeting mine again. "It's been a while."

I nodded. "Me too. I've never—"

"We'll go slow." He cut me off, his lips finding mine again, devouring mine. All too soon, an all-consuming fire rose between us, burning his desire to go slow to ashes.

His hand unclasped my bra and pulled it free of me before settling on my breast. He felt like heaven, cupping, kneading, squeezing me. It sent an answering twinge deep to my core and made me come alive. I longed for his touch, there. I grabbed his hand and pushed it down to that yearning place between my legs, sacrificing the intense pleasure I'd felt as his fingers rubbed and tweaked my nipples. The sacrifice was short-lived, however, because he tore his mouth from mine and trailed kisses down my neck only to settle his mouth over my right nipple. The jolt of pleasure as his mouth suckled on my breast tore a moan from my lips. His mouth was better than his hand, a thousand times more pleasurable. I was lost to the emotions coursing through me, pushing me higher and higher toward the edge of a cliff I was happy to fall over.

Evan pulled away from me, sitting up suddenly. He pushed his underwear down his legs, kicking them off.

"I was wrong. We can go slow the next time around." He shook his head at me before turning his attention back to the condom he was ripping open.

I giggled at the hilarity of it even as I nodded, my breath catching in my throat. Yes, next time, all night. Over and over. I wanted Evan for an eternity. Butterflies warred with hot lava in my stomach. I missed his hand on my core, his mouth on my nipple. I reached for him just as he leaned toward me.

His firm, hard body pressed against mine, claiming mine. Pain and pleasure collided.

I felt him stiffen. I shook my head. "Don't stop."

I cupped his cheeks, pulled his lips toward mine, kissed him—slowly, completely—even as that heat exploded again inside of me, driving me crazy.

"Please, move. Evan, I need you to move."

"Easy, baby," he whispered against my lips, but his blessed hips swiveled, sending more pleasure than pain shooting through me. I gasped. I bent my legs at the knees, driving him deeper, tearing an answering groan from him.

We were suddenly lost in a rhythm new to us but as old as time. We moved together, chasing the same rainbow, each stroke sending us higher and higher. He pushed, and I went willingly. And when he threw his head back, a groan tearing free from his lips, I fell over that cliff and floated somewhere between paradise and reality. Tears filled my eyes and fell down my cheeks.

I love you.

The words hovered on my lips as I floated back to myself. I opened my eyes to find Evan lying next to me, his arm draped around my waist. I felt hot all over. I buried my face in the crook of his neck, avoiding his gaze.

"You're mine now, you know that right?"

His words did something funny to me. I looked into his eyes and saw the emotions shining in them. "I'm glad you were my first."

"I am, too."

He kissed me then, softly, deeply, before he pulled away from me. I watched him walk toward his bathroom with sleepy eyes. A moment later, he was back and pressing a warm washcloth to my core. I let him clean away the last of our lovemaking without a shred of self-consciousness. Minutes later, Evan was back, lying by my side. He pulled me against him, settling me against his body. His arms tightened against my chest, holding me tight.

I felt safe, wrapped in the cocoon of his arms. Slowly, as my eyes drifted shut, I had the realization that lying next to him in his arms was a place I never wanted to leave.

20

Christina

$\mathcal{T}$he weeks following our Napa Valley weekend were something out of a fantasy. Evan and I spent every waking minute together. If I wasn't at the hospital, I was at his house, wrapped in his arms, exploring all the different aspects of lovemaking with him.

We had a lot of time to make up for, and we were both eager. I could feel the sappy smile on my face, but I didn't give a damn. I reached for his hand and squeezed it affectionately as we walked through the front lobby of my building.

It helped that most of the media hoopla surrounding our relationship had died down since our return from Napa Valley. I think Derek McKnight's new relationship with a certain supermodel fascinated the media and the public. I didn't mind one bit. Evan and I were both enjoying the break from the tension that came from not being in the media spotlight.

"Hello, Christina."

I glanced over my shoulder, my steps halting. A man in his early fifties stood behind us. He was dressed in jeans and a polo shirt. His salt-and-pepper hair was neatly cut and brushed back. He was shorter than Evan, just a little taller than me. The man took a step closer to us. He had my almond-shaped eyes.

I felt the ground move beneath my feet, and I stumbled, swaying toward Evan. I gasped and covered my mouth to stop any other sound from escaping.

"It's me."

"Who are you?" Evan pulled me closer against his side.

"I'm her father. Mike."

I glanced around the lobby as panic crawled up my throat.

"Over here." Evan inclined his head in the direction of the alcove with the vending machine, a table, and a couple chairs. My feet felt like lead as he led me over to the more private area.

"You're as beautiful as your mom."

Tears stung my eyes. I felt like I was in the deep end of a pool, and I couldn't break the surface no matter how hard I kicked.

"What do you want?" Evan demanded.

The man glanced at Evan before his eyes flickered to mine again. He took a step toward me. I stepped back. He stopped abruptly. Evan shifted, pulling me closer against him. He wrapped an arm around my waist and my shoulder, turning me into his body

"Christina, I'm sorry."

I breathed deeply. I took a breath and then another as this stranger continued speaking.

"I'm sorry, angel. I wanted you to know that I'm sorry for

walking out on you and your mom all those years ago. I was in a bad place. But I'm clean now. Five years sober. I just wanted to tell you so, you know."

Evan's arms tightened around me. "Let's go," he whispered in my ear, turning us away.

"Please, just give me a minute of your time." The man stepped into our path, trying to block us.

"Not tonight," Evan declared.

I closed my eyes, wanting to be anywhere but there.

"Where are you staying?" Evan asked.

"Five blocks from here. A motel on Fannin and Main Street."

"Christina will reach out *if* she wants to. Until then, stay away from her."

My father said nothing. I felt the weight of his stare, and I opened my eyes to meet his. I always thought I'd inherited my exotic eyes from my mother, but now I saw them looking back at me. Whatever he was about to say in protest died on his lips when he saw my face. He nodded, backing out of our way.

Evan led me quickly toward the bank of elevators and jabbed furiously at the button. I glanced back at my father and found him still standing by the archway, watching us.

The minute the elevator doors closed, Evan pulled his phone out of his jeans pocket and typed a quick message to someone. I stared straight ahead at the steel doors. I couldn't think of anything to say. Evan ushered me out of the elevator and toward my apartment door. He took my keys from my shaking hands and unlocked the door. My apartment was in total darkness for a moment before Evan flipped the switch, turning the lights on.

I stepped out of my shoes, leaving them there in the middle of the hallway. I needed to lie down. Now. I walked to my bedroom and crawled onto my bed, curling onto my side and pulling the covers up to my chin.

Evan walked into my bedroom. He set my shoes down next to the door before walking toward my bed. I watched him sit on the bed and remove his shoes before lying down next to me. He wrapped his arm around my waist and pulled me against his chest.

I could hear his beating heart beneath my ear. The sound anchored me and made me feel safe. The rhythm of his heartbeat kept me grounded in the present despite the pain of the past I was feeling. I wanted to close my eyes and slip away from the encounter in the lobby.

"Christina?" He sighed my name even as his hands tightened around me.

I felt as if my whole world had caved in over my head. I needed to say something, but no words would come. I just wanted to pull the covers over my head. Nothing could have prepared me for coming face-to-face with my father. It was worse than being ambushed by a disparaging news article.

I'd felt on top of the world walking into the lobby with Evan tonight, only to find myself free-falling through the air with no soft landing in sight.

"I thought he was dead," I whispered. "Why else wouldn't he have come for me? All these years? I thought he had to be dead not to come."

"I'm sorry." Evan tightened his arms around me.

I buried my face against his chest. "I don't want to talk about it."

What was there to say? My father hadn't cared to look for me before I'd connected with Evan. I held no value for him. It was why he'd never sought me out in the five years he'd been sober. I didn't want to think about the timing of his sudden reappearance in my life or what it would mean for my relationship with Evan.

"Okay." Evan pulled me closer. He stroked my hair, taming my thoughts and my anxiety. I let his touch soothe my emotions and carry me away from the memory of my father. I closed my eyes and lost myself in sleep.

21

Evan

I stroked Christina's silky black hair until her breathing evened out and sleep claimed her. Slowly, gently, so as not to wake her, I extricated myself from her hold, picked up my discarded shoes, and walked out of her bedroom.

I gritted my teeth, biting back curse words. I could guess why her father had suddenly crawled out of his hole.

I pulled out my cell phone. Sure enough, there was a text from Nigel responding to my earlier request to find out everything he could about Christina's father. Nigel had already informed Tom, and they were both on it.

I was damned if I was going to let Christina's father hurt her. It didn't take a rocket scientist to figure out why he was back in town and eager to rekindle his relationship with her. It would be up to Christina, of course. But I was going to do everything in my power to make sure she wasn't hurt in the process.

I thought back to our weekend in Napa Valley. She'd whispered she loved me. Her words had jolted me out of the euphoria brought on by my release. I'd realized as I stared at her face that she hadn't known she'd said it out loud. She'd most likely been overwhelmed by the emotions of our love-making. Her words had sunk deep into my soul, however. They had felt like a key unlocking a door to a part of myself that I'd locked away for the longest while. I'd lain next to her, unable to respond. But there were several moments since then that I'd found myself wanting to tell her that I loved her.

It was the way she cared for me. The way she put me first. I never felt like a meal ticket when I was with Christina. I didn't feel like Evan the famous football player or the billionaire son of Paul and Brandy Kennedy of Kennedy Enterprises. I just felt like myself. And there wasn't a part of me that she wanted to change. She loved me. All of me. And I loved her. All of her. Her wit, her humor, her kindness, her toughness, her vulnerability, her passion. I loved all of her. She was perfect for me. And it was my deepest desire to protect her. I wasn't about to let anyone hurt her, especially her absent, long-lost father.

22

Christina

*T*wo days had passed since my father had shown up. I still felt like I was underwater, and I couldn't break through to the surface no matter how hard I kicked. I put the clipboard back in the holder on the wall and walked away from my patient's room. My father's sudden appearance had the effect of tilting my world.

I'd always assumed that if he was alive, I would have heard from him by now. Ten years in CPS. He hadn't once come for me. Hadn't they tried to reach him? I'd just always assumed it was because he was dead. Why else hadn't he come for me? Why had it taken him this long to find me? Why now?

I didn't want to think the worst of him, but he'd walked out on my mom and me without a backward glance. Mom had been sick, too. It hadn't stopped him from leaving her. Now he was back, wanting a relationship with me. Was I the draw? Or was my relationship with Evan the reason why he'd turned up all these years later. Was I supposed to give him the benefit of the doubt?

He'd walked out. He'd made the decision all those years ago. I did not owe him anything.

"Hello, Christina."

His voice startled me out of my thoughts about him. I blinked twice and realized that I hadn't conjured him up. He was indeed standing in front of me. He had walked up the moment I'd stepped behind the front desk, which meant he'd been in the lobby, waiting for my return.

I wanted to ask him what he wanted. I glanced around the lobby instead. No one was paying any attention to us. I focused back on him.

His salt-and-pepper hair was neatly brushed back, high on top and low on the sides. He didn't look a day over forty, even though I knew he had to be in his fifties. I supposed there were similarities between us in the way we looked. I felt zero connection to him, however. He could have been just another person approaching the front desk.

"How may I help you?"

"Christina, please, just give me a few minutes of your time. I just want explain."

"You don't owe me any explanations."

"Please, just a moment of your time."

I glanced around the reception area again. This time, my eyes connected with the security guard's, who was watching us intently. I shook my head and then smiled at the man standing in front of me. I didn't want the guard to come over. I didn't want to create a scene.

"Not here. You can come to my apartment tonight. Seven o'clock. We can talk then."

He nodded, smiled. "Okay. Tonight then."

I sat in my chair and busied myself on the computer. I

didn't look up again until I felt him walk away. I didn't want him in my apartment, but I didn't want to listen to him here in the lobby, and I didn't want to take a break outside in the courtyard to speak with him either, lest we make the news cycle.

"Christina," I looked up at the sound of Amanda calling my name. She was standing next to me, the phone in her hand. She replaced it in the cradle.

"Chief Nancy wants to see you in her office."

I frowned. What could it be? I got up from behind the front desk and walked out of the lobby. My heart beat a mile a minute as I walked down the hall toward Chief Nancy's office. Her office door was open, and she was sitting at her desk, pen in hand, writing on a notepad. I knocked on the open door.

"Chief, you wanted to see me?"

"Yes, Christina. Please come in."

She indicated the chair in front of her desk. I sat, folded my hands in my lap, and waited.

"How are you doing?"

I frowned. "I'm good, thank you." Had someone filed a complaint about me? I knew I had been preoccupied lately with my father's sudden appearance, but I certainly hadn't let it affect my job. Had I?

"Good, I'm glad to hear it. I don't want to interrupt your shift more than necessary. Christina, I just wanted to let you know that the fellowship committee made its decision earlier this afternoon. It was unanimous. Congratulations, you've won the fellowship."

"Really?"

"Really!"

Laughter of pure joy bubbled past my lips, and I slapped my hand over my mouth to contain it. For the first time since my father's appearance, I felt like everything was going to be okay again. I felt as if I'd taken a leap out of a plane and I was soaring! No longer standing still in limbo, but that everything I'd been working for all this while was suddenly attainable. I felt like I'd leveled up.

And there was one person I couldn't wait to tell.

"You're a superb nurse, Christina. You're dedicated, alert, analytical, and compassionate. All the things we want in our recipient. I see you doing very well on the administrative side. Learn all you can this upcoming year. You've got a bright future ahead of you."

I walked out of Chief Nancy's office floating on air. Joy made my heart take flight. There was only one person I wanted to speak to right now. Reaching for my phone, I dialed Evan's number.

He answered on the second ring. "Christina?"

"I got it! I got the fellowship!"

Evan's answering whoop had me pulling the phone away from my ear and laughing out loud at his enthusiastic response.

"This is cause for celebration. You and me, dinner tonight!"

I thought of my dad coming over at seven o'clock, and I didn't think I would feel like a night out on the town after our conversation.

"How about takeout? My place at seven thirty?"

"You got it. I'll pick it up. Text me what you're in the mood for."

"Evan..." I paused. Those three huge words rang in my heart. Instead, I swallowed and told him my other truth. "You helped me put the application together. I can safely say I wouldn't have done it if it hadn't been for you working through my fear of failure with me. So, thank you. Thank you so much!"

"You're welcome, baby. I'll see you tonight."

I hung up feeling like I was on top of the world. I shot off a text to Nadia and Fey and was immediately inundated with smiling emojis and exclamation marks. For the first time in a long time, my life felt full, complete.

23

Evan

"Something happen?"

"Christina got the fellowship."

"Good for her."

Jake walked behind my bar and grabbed a bottle of cold water from the fridge.

"Yeah. I'm proud of her."

I watched him twist the cap off and on and off again before taking a deep swallow of the water. I swear, sometimes Jake had OCD tendencies and he didn't even realize it. Always when he was anxious about something.

"Jake, what's going on? You're over at my house at four in the afternoon. I'm not complaining—it's always great to see you—but typically you call. Unless all hell's breaking loose. So what gives?"

"You know, timing's everything."

"Just spill it."

"I got a call from Frank Dempsey this afternoon."

Every muscle in my body went tight. "From the 49ers?" It was a dumb question. The only Frank Dempsey I knew was the head coach for the San Francisco 49ers, and which other Frank Dempsey would be calling for me anyway? Wait, why was he calling for me?

"Evan, he wants you to play for him."

I leaned against the back of the sofa.

"I floated the idea that you might be interested."

"What? My life is here. My family—"

"It was before Christina. We'd just entered conversations with MacMillan Brothers, and it made sense to explore a move to San Francisco and the 49ers. I didn't expect them to entertain it seriously. But, Evan, they are. It's a good offer."

"My life is here."

"It's a chance to get the ring. Think about it. The team's got the best quarterback in the NFL right now. And Dempsey's a man on a mission. It's the chance to make it to the Super Bowl. Win a ring, at least one, before you retire."

Now it was my turn to walk around the bar and grab a bottle of water. Unscrewing the cap, I brought the bottle to my mouth and took a long drink.

Back in college, when my football career was just starting, I dreamed of Super Bowl rings. It was the goal. After the rape accusation, I just wanted to play football with any team that would give me a chance. The goal was the game and playing my heart out for as long as I could, if they would let me.

Now, fate was handing me the ultimate opportunity. Did I dare say yes?

"At least take the meeting."

I met Jake's stare across the bar.

"Dempsey's expecting you tomorrow."

"An interview?"

"A meeting. Nothing's written in stone. It's just you, meeting with Dempsey and a couple of his coaches."

"Shit, Jake. Are you for real?"

"Hey, we're not making any moves yet, alright? It costs you nothing to have a face-to-face. It could mean everything for your future."

He was wrong. I felt it deep in my gut. This opportunity that he'd landed me had the potential to wreck my future—the future that had been budding these last couple months with Christina. Not to mention how my teammates would react if they found out I was even entertaining this idea.

"You owe it to yourself to see where this goes. Take the meeting. Get a feel for it. You have nothing to lose and everything to gain."

Nothing to lose? Christina's smiling face floated before my eyes. I needed to talk to her. I needed to run this by her. This would affect her greatly, more than my mom and my dad, Char, or Max. I needed to speak to Christina.

Like a lost man wandering the dessert who'd suddenly found water, I couldn't get enough of Christina. Since Napa Valley, being with her gave me new life. I felt richer, fuller, and my life seemed so much more worth it.

I couldn't play football forever. I was twenty-four. I still felt like I had another three or four good years left in me. But now was the time to put my deals in place. Whereas before I had approached the deals Jake was putting together for me with a sense of finality, as if they heralded the end of my professional life, I now felt excitement for the new chapter they signified in my life. But this thing with the 49ers was a game changer.

"Set the alarm behind you."

"Evan!" Jake called after me as I walked out of the library.

I paused. Timing was everything. If this had happened earlier in the year, I would have been over the moon. But now, being with Christina, I couldn't imagine my life without her.

"I'll let you know, okay? I just need a moment to think about it. I'll text you."

I walked out the side door and into the garage. I grabbed the keys for the MC20 off the hook and climbed in. I was super early for dinner at Christina's, but I didn't care. I needed to get away from Jake, from this moment. He'd only done what I was paying him the big bucks to do—advance my career. Yet, it seemed like he'd sabotaged my relationship with Christina.

Was I being real? Four years with no relationships. How the hell was Jake to know I would have found someone I liked and wanted to pursue? This thing with Christina had come out of the blue. I hadn't seen it coming. Jake had probably thought it was going to blow over. He hadn't anticipated that a move to San Francisco might be out of the question for me.

It would have been one thing if Christina was just with me for my money. She wasn't. She and I had formed a connection that went way beyond the trivial public relations ruse we'd entered to. She was real. This fake relationship that had started just for fun meant a hell of a lot to me now, and it was anything but fake.

I'd avoided relationships for years. I trusted very few people, and I avoided romantic entanglements at all costs. Christina was the first woman I could see myself in a relationship with. What would San Francisco do to us?

I didn't want to find out. My desire to stay and see where things could go with Christina was stronger than a chance at a Super Bowl ring.

I pulled my car over to the side of the road as shock hit me like a ton of bricks. I didn't want a life that didn't involve Christina. I *loved* her. I was head over heels, willing to give up a chance at a Super Bowl win in love with Christina.

I put the car back in gear, checked my mirrors, and pulled back into traffic. There was only one question now: what was I going to do about it?

24

Christina

The doorbell rang. My heart sank into my stomach. I opened the door and stepped aside so that my *father* could walk in. Nadia was in her bedroom. Fey was out with her latest fling. Nadia had said to text her if I needed the backup. I thought I could handle the man who had walked out on me without a backward glance. Besides, I didn't want to make a big deal about this. I wanted to hear what he had to say and then wish him farewell.

I glanced at my watch. We had just over thirty minutes before Evan got here, and I truly planned for my dad to be gone by then so Evan and I could celebrate my fellowship win.

"I'm listening," I prompted him.

"I'm sorry."

I nodded. "You've said so already. There's no changing the past, so no sense in dwelling on it. Right?"

"I was hoping there would be a place for me in your life now. I want to make up for the time we lost. I want us to spend some time together, get to know each other."

I watched the smile toying at his lips. I saw the self-assured way he stated his plans, and I wondered if I could ever be as bold as he was.

I had zero interest in spending time with him. I didn't know him from any stranger off the street. I wished there was some connection or some inkling of emotion that made this man feel like my father, but there was nothing. I didn't even feel curiosity about him. Just an emptiness. I wanted nothing to do with him.

"I don't want to waste your time, so I'll be honest with you. I'm glad you're sober and clean and you've turned your life around. But I don't have room in my life for a father now."

He nodded and looked away, his eyes darting around the living room. I suddenly felt a pang of sorrow, a moment of regret that I was bursting his bubble. I stamped down on the emotion, unwilling to open myself up to someone who had walked away from me and hadn't looked back.

"Okay, but do you have room for a friend?"

I didn't respond, and he continued. "I know I hurt you. I wish I'd been able to come back sooner. But I was sick. My addiction left me in no position to care for you. I got clean five years ago, but it wasn't until just recently that I was able to find you."

"Did you look for me? I've been here in Houston this whole time. You've been sober for five years. You could have come for me. Why didn't you?"

"I was ashamed. I didn't have anything to offer you. I was sure that you were settled in your life. I thought you were better off without me."

Perhaps I had been. Five years ago, I'd already formed my sister pact with Nadia and Fey. We were already on our own and fighting to establish our careers. Perhaps my father showing up unexpectedly would have thrown me for a loop. His presence may have derailed me.

And isn't he derailing you now?

I'd spent a lifetime avoiding relationships and deep commitments because I believed all men left. After all, my own father had walked out of my life. I'd used that wound to shape every interaction I'd ever had with a man. I was holding back with Evan, letting my fear of being abandoned dictate just how deep I got in with him.

Hell, I loved Evan. I was madly, deeply in love with him. But I had yet to tell him, show him. I doubted he knew just how much he meant to me. And Evan was a good man. A man worthy of being told how special he was and just how worth loving he was. I'd been holding back for fear that he would leave me. All because my father had left me.

Perhaps now, I could let it go. Forgive. Release it. Move on. My father had left me. But he'd also come back. Late, yes, but he was here.

"I forgive you," I whispered.

He exhaled on a rush and took a step toward me. I stepped back before he could touch me. I wasn't ready for that. I just wanted him to know that I didn't hate him and that I appreciated him showing up.

The doorbell rang. I glanced at my watch and frowned. I still had fifteen minutes before Evan showed up. I wasn't expecting anyone else though, so something told me Evan was early.

I pulled the door open.

"Hi," Evan greeted me with a huge smile. He had a takeout bag in one hand and a bottle of wine in the other.

Bending down, he kissed me deeply, his lips moving over mine in a way that told me maybe, just maybe, he cared for me too. He was smiling when he lifted his head.

I moved back and he stepped inside the apartment. I saw the exact moment when he saw my father standing there. The smile on his face froze over before disappearing slowly. Evan looked at me. I saw the questions in his mind.

"He stopped by to chat for a moment. He was just leaving."

Evan nodded. Then his shoulders relaxed and dropped away from his ears as he smiled politely. "Not on my account I hope."

"Well, actually, I'd love to have dinner with my daughter, if you didn't mind sharing," my father said with an easy smile.

I felt Evan stiffen next to me, but the polite smile didn't disappear from his lips. I frowned at my father, taken aback once more by his boldness. It seemed he had no hang-ups about asking for what he wanted. Again, I felt that old pain of being abandoned by him. I pushed it aside. Forgive and release.

"It's up to Christina," Evan said with a shrug.

I looked between the two men, feeling oddly caught in the middle and unsure of my next move. I wanted to spend the evening celebrating with Evan, but I didn't want to offend Mike, who was going out of his way to reconnect with me. I wished I could be as bold as Mike was and go with what I wanted, but I realized that I just didn't have the heart.

"Sure, looks like there's plenty for three."

"Great! Mind if I use your bathroom first?" Mike asked.

I pointed him toward the guest half bath and watched as he walked away. When we were alone, I took the bags from Evan.

"I'm so sorry. He stopped by the hospital today wanting to explain everything to me and I didn't want to discuss it at work, so I invited him to come over so we could chat. But it was before I found out about the fellowship and before we planned our dinner. I planned to have him gone by the time you showed up."

"Hey, hey, Christina, it's okay. You deserve to have your father clear the air between you two. Like I said, I don't mind. I can wait until he leaves to properly celebrate you getting the fellowship."

Evan wrapped his arms around me and pulled me against his chest. My heartbeat crescendoed and settled again. Tonight, after my father was gone, I would tell Evan how I felt about him. He was worth taking the chance.

Thirty minutes later, I wasn't so sure that I could wait. We were seated at the dining table, me at the head and Evan and my father on either side of me. Conversation had flowed between Evan and Mike. Evan asked questions and Mike answered them easy enough. It turns out that he had done odd jobs here and there over the past five years while he focused on his rehabilitation. He admitted he'd seen an article about my relationship with Evan and that's how he'd found out I was still living in Houston.

"So, how long are you staying for?" Evan asked.

"Hadn't thought about it really. Actually, I'm thinking of sticking around for a bit. Looking for a job now to help me make the transition to Houston." He smiled his easy smile again.

"How's that going?" Though Evan sounded polite, I knew his tone well enough to know he was wary of my father and his motives. I was just about to reach across the table and squeeze Evan's hand reassuringly, when the next words that came out of my father's mouth caused my stomach to fall uncomfortably and a sick, queasy feeling to rise upward toward my throat.

"I could use any help you can offer. A man like you must have connections. It's all about who you know, right? Like I said earlier, I've done just about everything. I'm like a jack-of-all-trades, you know. Not much I can't handle."

Evan's gaze met mine briefly, and I fidgeted in my chair. I wanted to die of mortification. I hated that my father had just asked Evan for a handout. It was so inappropriate.

"I'm sure you'll find something soon." I spoke softly before Evan could.

Evan's phone beeped once, twice, a third time. He reached for it reluctantly, glanced at the screen, and winced slightly.

"Someone's blowing up your phone," Mike stated unnecessarily.

I glared at him, wishing he would leave already. "Everything okay?" I asked Evan.

"Jake. I'll call him later."

As if Jake had heard Evan, he fired off two more texts in rapid succession.

"It's okay if you need to call him now." I smiled reassuringly at Evan.

He pushed his chair back from the table. "Yeah, I better do that. Excuse me for a moment."

I watched as Evan walked out of the dining room. Mike stood too, reaching for my plate. "Are you finished? I'll wash these up before I get going."

"You don't have to do that." I felt a rush of warmth at his thoughtfulness.

"Hey, you fed me. It's the least I can do."

"Okay then." I gave in with a smile.

I remained sitting at the table. Moments later, I heard the kitchen sink turn on. Mike really was doing the dinner dishes. Gradually, I became aware of Evan's voice as he spoke on the phone with Jake. The ring of tension was clear. I frowned. What was it? Another media attack? Was something wrong with one of his business projects? I heard Evan say that he didn't care and that he wasn't interested a couple of times, but it sounded like Jake was insisting that Evan ought to be. Mike shut the faucet off just as Evan promised Jake he would be there at six in the morning. I grimaced at the early hour, which meant he and I wouldn't have a lot of time together tonight.

"Well, I'd best be on my way," Mike said, walking into the dining room.

I stood, pushing my chair in. "Thank you for coming tonight. It was good to clear the air."

He nodded. "It was. I'll see you soon, kiddo."

"Okay." I laughed at the nickname. It hadn't been too bad having Mike here with Evan and me tonight. It felt almost like my boyfriend and I had just had dinner with my father, as opposed to dinner with the man who had fathered me biologically but abandoned me when I needed him the most.

I walked him to the front door. Evan was standing in the living room, staring out of the balcony doors. I felt a moment of trepidation. Whatever was going on between him and Jake was serious. I all but hustled Mike out of the apartment, closing the door and locking it.

"Evan, what is it?"

He took a moment to turn to face me. When he did, there was uncertainty in his eyes. "You're not the only one with good news tonight."

"Oh?"

"Jake told me this afternoon that the 49ers want me on their team."

I felt my knees go weak at his announcement. "Wait, you're moving to San Francisco?"

"I told Jake no. But he just called to tell me, unofficially, that they're willing to offer me a whole lot more than what I'm making now. Jake wants me to meet with them tomorrow morning. He thinks it'll be better for me if I turn them down in person."

I sat on the couch, feeling the blood draining from my head. That sick feeling of fear and anxiety had risen to my throat and was choking me.

Evan was moving to San Francisco.

He sat next to me, taking my hand in his and holding it between his two palms. "Jake and I will fly out tomorrow morning at six. I'll take the meeting. I'll thank them, and then I'll be back in time for you and me to have a late dinner."

I shook my head. This must be one hell of an opportunity for Jake to be so insistent. Wasn't Evan launching a business deal in San Francisco? It made sense for him to play football over there. Besides, I didn't know much about the NFL teams, but even I knew the 49ers were good. Super Bowl good.

I smiled, even though I could feel my heart falling away in tiny chips. "Congratulations."

Evan shook his head. He cupped my cheeks. "Baby, I'm not moving to San Francisco."

I nodded. He kissed me, his lips moving reassuringly, lovingly over mine. I wished I could believe him. But I'd fallen in love with him, and didn't the men I love leave? In the beginning, I'd expected it to happen with Evan too, but as we'd grown closer together, I'd let my guard down. I thought our love would stand a chance. I should have known better. Men left...me. And Evan would be no different.

25

Christina

I woke up the next morning alone in my bed. Sometime during the early morning, Evan had left, having a flight to catch. I glanced at the clock. It was after seven in the morning. He was most likely already airborne.

I needed coffee. Moments later, I was standing in front of our single brewer, watching my favorite mug fill with the fragrant black liquid. Nadia's bedroom door opened, and I heard her walk into the kitchen behind me.

"You okay?" She reached for a cup from the cupboard and came to stand next to me.

I shrugged.

Together, we listened to the machine hiss as it spilled the last of my brew into my cup. I tossed the spent pod in the garbage.

"Is Evan here?"

I shook my head as I poured milk into my coffee.

"Want to talk about it?"

Facing my friend, I said, "There's not much to talk about."

"I'm here if you change your mind."

I nodded. A few moments passed as we drank our coffee in silence. Nadia knew I wasn't a big talker. Between my father's unexpected return and Evan taking the meeting in San Francisco, I might need to take her up on the offer, however.

I hugged her briefly before walking into my room to take a shower and get dressed for work. Nigel was going to be here to pick me up soon.

I wondered what the latest development in Evan's life would mean for our relationship. Truthfully, most of the hoopla over that photo of us at Club Yes had died down. People accepted that we were in a relationship. Apparently, though, it was too tame of a relationship for them, and they had moved their interest elsewhere.

Our breakup would probably land somewhere below the fold. Nothing to cause a stir. Nothing to cry over. Except, I felt like crying. I'd fallen in love with Evan. Only a fool would have thought that I could spend time with a man like Evan, who was everything I'd dreamed about, and not fall in love with him. And I had been that fool.

Later, when Nigel knocked on the door, I was waiting for him. I opened it and felt a pang of sadness that this was coming to an end. I enjoyed the ride to work every day. It was nice not having to wait on the bus, being able to relax against the cool leather seat instead. I made a promise to myself that I would learn how to drive. I would be busy with the fellowship position, but I was going to do something about my lack of a driver's license.

"Nigel, you don't have to pick me up tonight."

He paused just in front of the hospital entrance. "It's my job."

It wouldn't be for longer. I nodded. Turning, I walked away. I didn't want to fight with Nigel or make things difficult for him either. This was a conversation I had to have with Evan anyway. There was no reason to pull Nigel into the middle of it.

I moved through my shift, determined to focus on my patients and their needs instead of wondering what Evan was up to in San Francisco. He'd promised me his meeting would change nothing. But, as the day moved on and there was still no word from him, I felt my anxiety climb.

I was pulling my bag out of my locker at the end of my shift when I felt someone's presence behind me. I turned, my heart in my throat.

"God, Becky, you scared me." I sighed in relief.

The other's woman's lips were drawn together in a tight line, no hint of a smile. Her eyes were cold, flinty. She looked pissed. She had yet to say something, just stood there staring at me.

"What's your problem?"

I felt the tension coiling in my stomach. It had been a while since I'd gotten into an altercation with someone. Not since I'd been a teenager facing down a bully in our group home. But right now, I had no doubt that Becky was seriously angry with me—fighting angry.

"*You're* the problem. You thinking you can use your boyfriend's name and his family's money to get the fellowship."

I laughed, though there was nothing funny about the accusation. "What in the world are you talking about?"

"You bought that fellowship win. Or rather you had your boyfriend's foundation do it for you. You thought none of us would find out, right? Because how would a bunch of nurses find out that they lost the opportunity of a lifetime because you had your boyfriend donate to the hospital."

I felt my world tip precariously and had to lean against my locker for support. "I don't know where you're getting your information but you're wrong."

"Don't you dare play innocent with me." Becky took a step forward, her voice rising an octave. I glanced around. The changing room was thankfully empty.

"My best friend works in the fundraising department. Besides, I was there that day Brandy Kennedy visited with the chief and made the donation. You had coffee with her after, and it wasn't even your break time. You're every inch the gold digger. You latched onto Evan Kennedy and all the money that family has, and you're milking it for everything you've got."

I opened my mouth to defend myself, but no words came out. I remembered Brandy's visit to the hospital. It had been right after the gala and the morning of that horrendous article that had painted me as a gold digger.

"That isn't how this went down, Becky. I promise you."

She scoffed in response.

I shook my head. "And if it is, I'll fix it."

I walked out the front door and caught the bus home instead of going to the garage to meet Nigel. I needed to speak to Evan, and I needed answers from his mother. She was head of the foundation, but I didn't dare approach her on this. The more I thought about it, the more I felt guilty of what Becky had accused me of.

His mother had been at the hospital, donating to the foundation. Had Evan asked her to do that to buy favor with the committee? Brandy liked me. She and I had a similar background and she empathized with me. She'd encouraged me in my relationship with Evan. Had she made the donation on her own without Evan's knowledge?

Money was nothing to Evan or his mother. The Kennedys had enough money and clout to sway the fellowship committee. Would they do it for me? If Evan wanted me to have the fellowship, would he have stooped to bribery to make it happen? My gut said no. I didn't know if Brandy had it in her either. But if they were doubtful of my ability to do it on my own, and they wanted the win because it made them look good, would they throw money at the situation then?

What in the world was I thinking? This was Evan. He didn't use money as a weapon, not like this. He was honest and fair and good. Becky was wrong. She had to be.

There was only one person who could reassure me now, but he was in San Francisco, most likely in a meeting that would tear us apart.

26

Evan

"That went well," Jake said, as we walked out of Levi's Stadium.

Jake had already called our driver, and the man and the car were waiting for us at the curb.

I nodded. It had gone great. Frank and his team were good. They'd laid it all out on the table. It would be a good opportunity. They were heading to the Super Bowl, and they wanted me along for the win.

I'd listened to them lay out their deal for me, and I'd listened to Jake make all the right demands and all the right noises. All the while, I'd wanted to be back in Houston with Christina.

"Let's go home, Jake."

I slid into the back seat of the car and scooted over so Jake could join me. If he was disappointed that, at the end of the meeting, I'd thanked the gentlemen and promised that Jake would be in touch, well, he wasn't showing it. I'd been upfront with Jake from the beginning. The timing was wrong. I wasn't looking to make a move to San Francisco right now.

We were five minutes from the airport when my phone vibrated in my pocket. I pulled it out and glanced at the screen.

"Shit." I showed Jake the name on the screen before answering.

"Ty, my man, what's up?" The last time I'd spoken to Ty had been the night I'd met Christina—when he, Nate, and I had gone to Club Yes during our boys' night out.

"You tell me, fuck face! Is it true? Are you meeting with the 49ers?"

My stomach heaved, and I clenched the phone tightly against my ear. I heard Jake swear under his breath, and I looked over at him. He was staring at his iPad, a look of anger on his stern face. I grabbed the device from his hands and read the news headline.

Evan Kennedy in talks to move to San Francisco 49ers. What does this mean for Chrisan?

"What are you talking about?" I squeezed my eyes shut and kept the emotion out of my voice.

"It's all over the news, dick face. You're in San Francisco negotiating with Frank Dempsey and his team. Man, I thought we were friends. Imagine my surprise seeing this shit on my newsfeed."

"It's crap, Ty. Someone got it wrong."

"Yeah, well, doesn't sound like it. According to the article I read, a credible source very close to you says you flew to San Francisco today to take a meeting."

I felt bile rise in my throat. I met Jake's eyes and saw the same anger and disbelief that I felt reflected there. He pulled out his cell phone and continued to read the article there.

"It's all bullshit, Ty. I'm not leaving the Texans. Houston's my home. Look, I got to let you go. I've got to get to the bottom of this."

"Alright, man. Hey, I'm sorry. Let me know if you need anything. Man," Ty added, "you can't catch a break with the media, can you?"

"Yeah, sucks to be me." I laughed, but I felt hollow inside.

Ty and I hung up. I leaned my head against the back of the seat. I didn't ask Jake how the hell this could have happened. We'd both been discreet about this visit. I hadn't even told my family about this.

"Christina." Jake whispered her name like an angry swear word.

"Watch it." I didn't like his tone.

"Are you kidding me right now?" He exploded, twisting in his seat to fully face me.

"It's my mess to deal with, okay?"

"The hell it is. Whose job do you think it is to clean this up?"

"I'll deal with Christina. You focus on shutting this down." I tapped on the screen and all but threw the iPad back at him. "I told you I wasn't interested in the 49ers. My answer is still no. This article doesn't change anything. In fact, when the season starts and I'm still playing for the Texans, it'll prove that their credible source didn't know shit."

"It's not that easy and you know it. She painted a target on your back. Training camp's going to be a bitch for you."

"So I get sacked a couple times. The guys will get over it

when they realize the article was wrong, just more media bullshit."

I rubbed my chest where an odd aching had started. I wasn't afraid of the backlash from my teammates. I meant what I'd said to Jake. The team would get over it once I proved my loyalty and convinced them that I had no intention of switching to the 49ers. No, the pain I was feeling came from being betrayed by Christina.

Why did she do it? Her smiling face filled my mind, and I felt the ache deep in my chest expand. How could she have sold me out? It made no sense, and it went against everything I knew her to be. Unless I'd made another mistake. Had she been using me? Was it that I didn't know her at all? Had I put my trust in a woman who had seized the first opportunity she got to sell me out?

She had the fellowship now. Was this her way of breaking up with me because she no longer needed me in her life?

"Fuck!" I yelled, punching the empty seat next to me.

I needed to be back in Houston so I could speak with Christina, find out where her head was at. Not almost two thousand miles away with a four-hour plane ride separating us.

Jake was busy typing on his phone. I heard him fire off a couple emails. In the few minutes we had before we pulled up at the airport, he was on the phone with a reporter, doing his best to shut the story down. I tuned him out.

I felt sick to my stomach. I wasn't sure how things had gone south so fast. But I was sure that the worst was yet to come—when I was back in Houston, confronting Christina over her betrayal of me.

27

Christina

Iopened the door and stepped aside to let Evan walk into the apartment. He moved past me, careful not to touch me. I frowned at his cold greeting. When he'd called and asked where I was, saying that he needed to speak with me, I'd told him to come to my apartment. Perhaps he'd heard the coldness in my voice. Or perhaps he already knew that I'd found out what he'd done.

"Where's Nadia, Fey?"

"Working late." I sat on the couch, folding my legs beneath me. Reaching for one of the soft pillows on the sofa, I pulled it against my stomach. "How did your meeting go?"

"How do you think it went?"

I felt my anger at what he'd done give way to confusion. "I would guess they offered you the deal of a lifetime, but your attitude tells me otherwise."

He paced in front of me like a large panther. He was dressed in black trousers and a black dress shirt that strained to contain his muscular arms, his wide shoulders and chest. He stole my breath even as I felt the betrayal over what he'd done.

"Did you do it?" I finally asked.

He stopped in front of me, with his hands balled into fists at his sides. He frowned, shook his head.

"Did you bribe the committee to give me the fellowship?"

"What are you talking about?"

"Please, just tell me the truth. I know you're used to getting your way. And maybe you thought you were doing me a favor. But it's just the opposite. You took that win away from me. It was supposed to me mine, but you threw money at the committee to get them to pick me, like you throw money at every situation to get it to go your way. Everyone knows you donated to the hospital to get them to pick me for the fellowship. They hate me."

He took a step away from me and pressed his hand against his chest, rubbing it as if he ached there. A moment later, he fell into the sofa chair at his back.

"So that's why you did it?" He bowed his head in his palms, then was silent.

What the hell was he talking about? I shook my head, realizing I didn't even care because, just then, it hit me like a ton of bricks that he hadn't denied my accusation.

Anger rose like a tidal wave flooding out of me. "I thought you helped me fill out the application because you believed in me. But the joke was on me, right?"

He lifted his head, and my heart slammed into my throat at the look of pain in his eyes. He looked devastated, and my anger and pain seemed to take a back seat to the look of desolation on his face. I wanted to crawl across the space separating us and tell him it was okay.

"I did believe in you, Christina." His voice was soft, flat, lifeless.

"Then why did you do it? Why did you have your family foundation pay the hospital to give me the fellowship?"

"Mom donates to the hospital every year after the gala. This year's donation was no different. It had nothing to do with your fellowship. And every year, I match my mom's donation to the hospital. My private giving was nothing new." He spoke so matter-of-factly.

I searched his eyes and saw the truth there in his brown depths. Yes, the Kennedys had donated to the hospital, but it hadn't had anything to do with me. The timing was a coincidence. It had been nothing but circumstances strung together to tell a story that Becky and her friend wanted to hear.

Tears of relief flooded my eyes. I exhaled and reached for him. He stood abruptly, side-stepping my outstretched arms. I watched, my feet refusing to work, as he walked to the door.

"Evan." His name fell in a whisper from my lips.

He grabbed the door handle, leaned his head against the door. I stood up, unsure of myself. He stood with his rigid back to me, his hand on the doorknob, his head bowed against the front door. Was he leaving? Everything about his behavior screamed at me to keep my distance. I believed him when he said the donation had nothing to do with me getting the fellowship. Yet the air in the room still felt tense around us, as if the argument wasn't over.

"How much did they pay you to sell me out?"

His words filled the room. They were full of pain. He still stood with his back to me and his hand on the doorknob, but he straightened his back suddenly, pulling himself to his full height. When he turned, there was no trace of emotion on his face.

My heart stuttered and stopped before racing into a too-fast rhythm. I shook my head, not knowing what he was talking about.

"I wished you'd just asked me about the fellowship. It hurts that you would believe the worst about me and my family. It kills me that you would try to ruin me, ruin my career to get back at me. You accused me of bribing the committee to get you the fellowship. If I had done that, at least I'd have done it for you. So you would have your dream. What you did was spiteful and mean. It was low, dirty. The worst betrayal, Christina. And I won't lie. It hurts."

He pulled the door open but then shut it again. "And you know what's worse? I trusted you. No, more than trusted you. I was falling for you. I was willing to choose you over San Francisco. Because I thought there was something real here. Thanks for showing me who you are before..." He paused, shook his head. "I don't have to tell you that I never want to see your fucking face again."

Evan yanked the door open and walked out, slamming it shut behind him. Confusion, pain, and disbelief converged and flooded through my veins, causing me to shake like a tree caught in a hurricane.

"What?!" I screamed at the empty room. There was no answer. I replayed Evan's words in my head, tried to figure out how the tables had turned so effortlessly so that he was the one angry with me, accusing me of betraying him.

This had something to do with San Francisco. And perhaps the media? He'd asked how much money they'd paid me to betray him. I reached for my phone and opened my web browser.

I gasped as I read the headline. I fell to the couch, my

feet giving way. I read the article about Evan flying to San Francisco to take the meeting with the 49ers. It was rampant with speculation that he was leaving the Texans and moving to San Francisco.

I knew the story didn't come from Evan's camp. In fact, he'd decided on the meeting last night when Jake had called him. He'd promised he was flying out the next morning for the meeting but still coming home in time to have dinner with me. He'd had no intentions of accepting the offer, so it didn't make any sense that he would want it in the papers. In fact, it did more damage to him with the Texans, and why would he want to do that with nothing to gain?

He thought I'd sold the story to the media. He trusted Jake, and he knew he hadn't done it. I suspected it was just the three of us that had known about the meeting. It wasn't me, though. My heart demanded that I try to reach him, to tell him that it wasn't me, that I hadn't been the leak. But oddly, I remained on the couch, the phone in my hand, my heart broken in a million pieces.

I sat utterly still, unable to make a move. Evan had been so angry with me. He'd believed me capable of hurting him so deeply out of my own spite. He didn't know me any better than I knew him. What were we doing? This thing between us had started on the premise of a lie. Perhaps it was best that it ended now, on the premise of another lie.

I stood, suddenly bone wearily tired. I walked to my bedroom and shut the door behind me. As I crawled into bed and pulled the covers over my head, I had one final thought: eventually all men did leave. They simply left me.

28

Evan

$\mathcal{T}$he month of July brought three-digit temperatures and humid, rainy days. Luckily, the stadium's roof was closed and the air-conditioning was on full blast. Training camp had started a week ago, and it was a bitch.

Even though weeks had separated the start of training from that flash-in-the-pan article about me moving to San Francisco, which had quickly been denied by both the 49ers press team and mine, I'd still faced some blowback.

I'd gotten sacked so many times, it was hugely suspect, especially considering that I wasn't the fucking quarterback and hadn't been anywhere near the ball. I'd taken it all in good stride though, and I felt like my teammates had almost gotten it out of their systems.

The physical pain was nothing compared to the ache in my chest that just wouldn't quit. It felt like someone was tightening a screwdriver through my heart. The twisting and gnawing had me rubbing my chest often. It stemmed from Christina's betrayal. I was sure of it.

Damn! I'd fallen hard for her. I'd told her I was glad I'd found out what a lying, two-faced schemer she was before I'd fallen in love with her, but the truth was it had already been too late. I had already fallen in love with her. Was still in love with her.

It didn't help that I understood why she had sold me out. She'd been hurt, thinking that I'd betrayed her. No doubt someone had approached her and, in a moment of weakness, she'd thought to fuck me over. I should have been angry over what she'd done. The thought of her jeopardizing my career to hurt me should have made me hate her more than I'd ever hated anyone. Instead, I just felt that damn tightening in my chest. My fucking heart was breaking. There weren't enough hits from my teammates that could take that pain away.

Worse, my family was also feeling the weight of Christina's betrayal. I'd tried to pretend all was well, but after a few family dinners without Christina in attendance, I'd bitten the bullet and told them about the San Francisco fiasco. My mom had been hurt the worst, I think. She'd been rooting for Christina and me. Char had felt certain there was another explanation, but my dad and Max had sat in silence, backing me up. Like me, they remembered four years ago and the spiteful things people could do when they were hurting. Like me, they understood why she'd done it. Like me, they knew I had to cut her loose. It was for the best.

"Hey, man, how you holding up?"

I glanced at Ty, who'd run up on my side. "As good as can be expected. When do you think you guys are going to lay off?"

Ty smirked. "I think we're about done."

I shook my head, wishing I cared. Yeah, that pain in my chest dwarfed everything else.

"What are you doing tonight? Nate and I are heading out to Club Yes. Why don't you come?"

My stomach pitched and rolled. "I don't think so."

"Come on. It'd be good."

"Got plans already. Rain check though, okay?" I jogged off before Ty could push me harder.

If I never saw Club Yes again, it'd still be too soon. In fact, there were very few places I could be without memories of Christina flooding my mind. Even certain rooms in my house were off-limits.

It was maddening, mostly because my body still reacted to thoughts of her, despite her betrayal. It would help if I could hate her. It would help if my damn chest didn't ache so much. Damn, it would help if I didn't still want her. Need her. Love her.

"Fuck!"

29

Christina

The weeks following Evan's exit from my apartment and my life passed in a blur. I'd spent most of the time at the hospital, working my shifts and picking up extra shifts where I could. Today, I climbed on the bus and picked a seat in the back. It was only Wednesday, but I was glad to be getting off, since I was suddenly aware of how tired I was. The good news was that I started my fellowship on Monday, and so I'd taken Friday, Saturday, and Sunday off. One more workday before my very long weekend.

Finding out Evan had believed the worst in me, just like I had believed the worst in him, left me alternating between anger and hurt. I'd spent my lifetime not needing anyone except Nadia and Fey. Somehow Evan had crept through my barriers. I missed everything about him. He'd been my haven the past couple months. I wanted to fight for him rather than let him go. But at the same time, I felt like our breakup was for the best and I ought to let him go.

I got off the bus and walked the few steps to my condo building. I waved at Phillip at the door as I walked past him.

"Good evening, Miss Christina. How are you doing today?"

"Exhausted!" I tossed behind me as I continued to the elevators. I heard his laughter and smiled.

Moments later, I was letting myself into my apartment. The silence told me that I was alone. Nadia was working late and Fey had been spending a lot of time lately with her latest boyfriend. She wasn't ready to introduce him to us yet, but I suspected she was serious about him, because I hadn't ever known her to spend so much time with one guy.

I was walking toward my bedroom when the doorbell rang. I paused, my heart leaping in hope. I rushed to the door and opened it, only to feel disappointment rushing in. It wasn't Evan.

"Mike, hi." I hadn't seen my father in weeks. Not since that dinner with Evan, and truthfully, I hadn't even given him a second thought, consumed as I was by my breakup with Evan.

"Hey, kiddo, mind if I come in?"

I stepped aside and held the door open for him to walk in. I pulled the door shut behind me and leaned against it, needing the support. "It's been a while. I thought perhaps you'd left town."

"Not quite yet. How've you been?"

I frowned, moving away from the door, heading for the kitchen. I opened the refrigerator and grabbed a bottle of water. "Can I get you something?"

"Nah, I'm good. Thank you, though."

I walked back toward him, sitting in one of the stools in

front of the kitchen bar top. I watched him closely. I suspected I had an idea where this was going. We hadn't connected the way Mike had originally intended when he'd come into town. Weeks had passed since we'd last seen each other. Though we'd cleared the air between us, there didn't seem to be anything there for us to build a relationship on.

He glanced at his watch as if he had someplace else to be. I caught sight of it as he lowered his hand, and the air left my chest in a rush. In that moment, I understood everything. I met his eyes. He shifted uncomfortably before sliding his gaze away from mine.

"That's a nice watch, Mike." It looked like one that Evan wore. It was obviously expensive and new to my father. He hadn't been wearing it the night he'd been here for dinner. The night before Evan left for San Francisco.

The night Mike was washing dishes in the kitchen while Evan was arguing with Jake about the meeting with the 49ers the next day.

"You told the press about Evan's meeting with the 49ers."

"I didn't mean to cause trouble for you. I needed the cash." He shrugged. "I'm leaving town. Catching a bus to Dallas tonight. That's what I came here to tell you. I didn't want you thinking I'd just up and left you again."

I scoffed in disbelief. Was he for real? I pushed the hurt aside and focused on what I most wanted to know. "Did you mean anything you said that night? About wanting to reconnect with me. Or did you only come here hoping for a paycheck, which you obviously got." I pointed at his watch.

"I didn't mean to cause trouble for you, Christina."

"Funny, I don't believe you." I jumped off the stool and walked to the door, pulling it open. "You know what? I don't even care to know why you came. You're right—there's nothing here for you. Hope you have better luck in Dallas."

I held the door open for him, waiting for him to leave. He looked like he was going to protest, like there was something he wanted to say to me. I shook my head and moved away from the door, leaving it open for him.

I'd let him into my life even though I should have known better. Worse, I'd given him access to Evan. And he'd hurt Evan just as he'd hurt me. This time, the pain Mike had caused was my fault.

I heard the door close and when I turned around, I was alone in the apartment. I felt the cry rising in my throat and clamped my hand over my mouth.

Evan had never betrayed me. He hadn't ever doubted that I deserved the fellowship. He'd only been good to me, only ever been on my side. I'd lost him because I'd allowed fear and my damned insecurities to cause me to believe the worst in him.

I hadn't sold him out, but he still was right. I had jumped to the wrong conclusion about his hand in my fellowship win instead of giving him the chance to explain himself. I had condemned him, choosing to believe the worst about him and his family, instead of trusting who I knew him to be.

Evan deserved better than me. He deserved someone who would love him with all they had. Not someone so damned imperfect, so filled with fear and insecurities that she had nothing worthwhile to give him.

It was for the best that he had dumped me. I loved him enough to respect that he never wanted to see me again.

30

Evan

𝒥 was leaning against my kitchen island, drinking a cup of coffee, when Nigel and Jake walked in. I glanced at the clock on the wall—barely nine thirty on a Thursday morning.

"What gives?" I asked, deciding not to beat around the bush.

Nigel placed a folder on the island next to me. Jake walked to the coffee machine, grabbing a mug as he went.

"You wanted me to keep an eye on Christina's father."

I shook my head. That was before. I glanced at the folder as I took a sip of my coffee, ignoring my building curiosity.

"He caught a bus for Dallas last night."

"He's gone?"

Nigel nodded. "He got a huge payout before leaving town, though. The folder contains pictures of him visiting a jewelry store, shopping at a high-end boutique, and buying a round of drinks at the bar down the street from Christina's condo, before paying her a visit."

"Where'd he get the money from?"

Nigel opened the folder himself and pulled out a photo, holding it out to me. I reached for it, my eyes dropping to the image. Christina's father was standing on the street accepting a small envelope from a man I didn't recognize.

"Curry Garza." Jake answered my unspoken question. "He's a reporter."

I frowned. "Tell me what this means." I looked up at Nigel, then turned to face Jake.

Jake was leaning against the counter, the coffee cup halfway to his mouth. "Looks like her father told the press about your meeting in San Francisco. I have no idea how he found out to begin with."

For the first time in weeks, I felt that screwdriver feeling ease in my chest. It hadn't been Christina. I took a deep breath, feeling like I could breathe for the first time since leaving her.

"He was there with Christina and me the night before we flew out for the meeting. He must have overheard my phone conversation with you."

I'd been an idiot! I'd suspected the worst of her, instead of giving her a chance to defend herself. I'd gone with a theory born out of my fear and insecurities, and I'd blown the best thing that had ever happened to me.

There was no doubt in my mind—Christina was the best thing in my life. I'd been miserable without her. I couldn't breathe deeply. The days dragged without her. My home, my library, my pool, even the damn kitchen—every space felt empty without her there.

"Where is she now?" I asked Nigel. He wasn't driving her

anymore, but I knew he and Tom were still keeping tabs on her.

"The hospital."

I didn't waste any time getting over to Mass Memorial. I saw her the minute I walked through the front doors. A shot of desire pumped through my veins. She was standing behind the front desk, her head bowed as she wrote on a chart. Her hair fell in loose, dark waves around her. She looked thinner than she had the last time I'd seen her. I took a step toward her, unable to resist her pull. I saw her go still a moment before she looked up, her gaze connecting with mine.

Her beautiful chocolate-brown eyes went wide as she flattened her palm against the desk, leaning against it. I closed the distance between us until only the desk separated us.

"What are you doing here?" Her voice was low in the now quieting lobby. There were dark shadows under her eyes.

"I accused you of something without taking the time to learn the truth. I'm sorry."

"You know it wasn't me?" she asked.

I nodded.

Her eyes darted around the lobby, taking in our audience. She walked around the desk, closing the distance between us.

"I'm sorry. Mike must have heard you while he was doing the dishes." Her voice was soft, apologetic.

"You knew?"

She nodded. "I figured it out."

"Why didn't you tell me?"

"What difference would it have made?"

"Christina." I took a step closer to her. Shaking my head,

I continued. "It's okay. It's not even important. I let an old fear cloud my judgment. I should have known that you would never sell me out for money. I should have looked for another explanation myself instead of believing the worst."

I stroked her face and tipped her chin up so that she met my eyes. I saw the tears swimming in hers.

"I'm guilty of doing the same thing. I'm so sorry I accused you of bribing the fellowship committee. I listened to a jealous lie, and I ran with it instead of trusting you."

Now the tears spilled over and splashed against my fingers. She moved her head so that I was no longer cupping her cheeks. She swiped at her wet cheeks and looked away.

"Can we try again?" I asked.

Shaking her head, she looked up at me. "It's too late," she whispered.

I felt my heart dip at the look of despair in her eyes. I held my breath, waiting for her to continue. She remained silent.

"I love you."

Her head snapped up, and she met my stare with brown eyes made darker by her emotions. She frowned, her mouth dropping open to form a perfect little O.

"I love you, Christina. Madly, deeply. I'm in love with you. I should have told you weeks ago. I think I fell in love with you the moment I saw you walking toward me in that restaurant. I wanted to know everything about you. And when we spent time together that first weekend, I realized you were perfect for me. You saw me, not my money or my family name. You liked me, the man. I should have told you then. But I was afraid, and maybe a little stubborn. I didn't want to trust that what we have was the real deal.

"But it is! I know that now. It's been hell without you. I miss everything about you, and nothing in my life matters because you're not with me. Being apart from you these last few weeks, nothing else matters as much as it did with you. I love you."

Christina wrapped her arms around my neck, hugging me tightly against her. I felt her tears falling on my skin. "I love you too, Evan. I was scared to love you. I thought you would leave me eventually. And when you did, I realized it was because I pushed you away. I let you walk out of my life without a fight. I love you, and I should have told you. You mean so much to me. More than money or fame. More than any dream. You matter to me. I love you."

"Say you'll be mine, Christina. Whether we're in private when it's just the two of us, or here, in the middle of the hospital lobby when I'm kissing you, and people are video-taping us, and I don't give a damn because you're mine. I want the whole world to know I'm yours."

Christina laughed, leaning closer to me. "You're kissing me in public?"

I kissed her then like I'd wanted to when I first walked through the doors and saw her. She sighed, opening her mouth for me. I barely heard the applause from our audience. I felt her give herself over to me, and I knew that whatever came our way, we would get through it together. We had to. Because I'd had life with Christina, and I'd had life without Christina, and having Christina was so much more worth it.

EPILOGUE

Christina

I stood next to Nadia in front of the bar in Evan's library, listening to Fey go on in hushed tones about the new guy in the condo down the hall from us. Across the room, Jake, Max, and Paul were deep in conversation. Brandy and Char were sitting on the couch. The television above the fireplace was on but muted, the post-game wrap-up droning on silently. Four months had passed since Evan came to the hospital and told me he was madly in love with me. Four whirlwind months of love and romance in a relationship that made me smile just thinking about it.

Football season had started, and Evan and his team were doing great. It was still early in the season, but some experts where hinting that the team had what it took to go further than they had before. I was happy for Evan, given that he had turned down San Francisco and one of the best teams in the league to stay in Houston with me. Most times, my girlfriends and I went to the stadium to watch him play, but tonight Char had proposed that we all watch here in the library. Sometime after halftime, Paul, Brandy, Max, and Jake had shown up. Now, we were waiting for Evan to come home from his winning game.

My fellowship was everything I'd imagined it would be. I was learning so much from shadowing some of the best doctors and nurses in the industry. I hadn't yet spent any of the grant money. It sat in an investment account, along with the fifty thousand that Evan had set aside for me when we'd started our fake romance. According to Matthew, Evan's financial guy, I was earning good dividends and well on my way to having a sizeable down payment for a very nice house.

No surprise, I'd yet to start house hunting. Between work, the fellowship, and Evan, my life felt full. I was okay waiting for things to settle down before I introduced house hunting into the mix. Besides, I was spending a lot of time at Evan's anyway, hence Fey's detailed report of her run-in with the new guy down the hall whom I had yet to meet.

I smiled as Evan walked into the library. Cheers and clapping erupted behind me as I walked over to him.

"What took you so long?" I teased.

Evan laughed as his mouth descended on mine. I let him kiss me thoroughly despite our family watching. We could have been standing in the middle of the stadium and I still would have let him kiss me. Letting Evan love me was easy. Loving him was my pleasure.

Evan let me go and went around the room, greeting the others. George soon appeared in the doorway to tell us that dinner was ready. Evan was standing with his father and Max, having a hushed conversation. They went quiet as I approached.

"Hey, are you ready to eat?"

Evan wrapped his arms around my waist. I saw the devilish hint in his eyes and blushed furiously.

"Actually, before we head off to dinner, Christina, there was something I wanted to run by you."

"What is it?"

I realized that the room had gone quiet, and Brandy and Char were smiling at me from the couch. Nadia and Fey were still leaning against the bar, but now Jake stood by Nadia's side and all three of them were watching me intently.

Evan suddenly went down on one knee. My gasp echoed throughout the library. I covered my mouth even as the tears filled my eyes. Was he about to—?

"Will you marry me?"

"Yes! Yes, I will."

Evan slipped a solitaire ring with a diamond the size of Texas on my finger. I laughed at the sight of it. There was no way I could go to work with it on my finger. But it was so beautiful, like the handsome man kneeling in front of me and pulling me into his arms.

"I love you, Evan Kennedy." I cupped his cheeks in my palms and kissed him as his arm wrapped tightly around my waist.

"I love you, Christina Kennedy. Now and always."

I planned to spend the rest of my life showing Evan just how much I loved him—And having him show me his love for me. Our relationship may have started out just for fun, but now we were both playing for keeps, and it had all been well worth the wait.

AUTHOR'S NOTE

I would be remiss if I didn't say thank you to my super supportive husband. Your encouraging words made all the difference.

Thank you to my wonderful editor, Kristen Womble of Passkey Publishing. You made the editing process so painless. I can't wait to work with you on the next one.

Thank you to Shari Ryan, MadHat Studios for the lovely cover! You hit it out the park.

Last but not least, a huge thank you to all of you for reading Love Worth Having. I hope you enjoyed Christina and Evan's story as much as I loved writing it. Please consider leaving an honest review on Amazon.

If you'll like to be notified when my next book releases, please visit:

https://cutt.ly/TR2eCCg

Thank you!

Kay Knolls

ABOUT THE AUTHOR

Kay Knolls writes contemporary romances that feature alpha males and strong heroines in steamy, emotional situations that always end in a happily ever after! Kay lives in Texas with her family. When she's not writing, she's usually reading a book, or at the beach, digging her toes in the sand.

Learn more about Kay on her website:
www.kayknolls.com

Made in the USA
Monee, IL
30 June 2022

98886673R00134